MARAUDERS

A Novel by
SAWYER PERRY

Based on the Screenplay by
MARK SAVAGE

Encyclopocalypse Publications
www.encyclopocalypse.com

First Edition (Trade), 2025
ISBN: 978-1-966037-34-7

Cover Artwork by Glitchborn Studios
Layout and design by Sean Duregger
Interior formatting by Mark Alan Miller and Sean Duregger
Edited by Mike Watt

FOREWORD

MARK SAVAGE

MARAUDERS was an eruption of anger at the Australian film industry at the time (1985), and the government's knee-jerk censoring (or banning) of cult films like THE TEXAS CHAINSAW MASSACRE (banned), LAST HOUSE ON THE LEFT (banned), THE HILLS HAVE EYES (cut), PIXOTE (banned), DAWN OF THE DEAD (cut to ribbons). The industry itself was mostly government-funded — or assisted — so there was pressure to please the sensibilities of bureaucrats. As a fledgling moviemaker, the idea of pleasing a bureaucrat whose idea of a perfect movie was MY BRILLIANT CAREER didn't sit well.

I conceived the project after a visit to French Island, a little backwater community outside of Melbourne that felt somewhat incestuous, like something out of STRAW DOGS. In retrospect, my reaction to the place was more felt than factual. I don't think anybody who lived there was doing much more than farming or cultivating their retirement, and nobody was laying a siege on a quiet homestead. Still, there *was* a war of ferry operators going on, and there is still an abandoned prison there that once held miscreants of various persuasions.

The project was written in the frosty woods of a timber town called Noojee. It lies just outside of Melbourne, and it's name is an Aboriginal word that means "place of rest." I was staying there for a week to shoot a training video for professional tree-fellers (bogans with chainsaws). Since this first feature would be starring my brother Colin and friends, it made sense to create a story that would maximize cinematic tropes such as fighting, f*******g, and swearing in a "bogan" world. In Australia and NZ, a bogan is an unsophisticated or unrefined person, and there is much humor to be found in bogan interactions. I wrote the first draft on a typewriter I brought with me, and I made corrections on the typed pages. The expletive-laden dialogue was fun to write, and its over-the-top nature gave the actors something to chew on. My inspiration for the dialogue was simply recalling conversations I'd had or heard over the years, especially when I was shooting corporate videos in Alice Springs, which was my own personal WAKE IN FRIGHT experience.

Australians are, by birth, a fairly anti-authoritarian breed, at least until they become parents or start paying taxes. This story, inspired by William Fruet's DEATH WEEKEND (a huge favorite of mine) and LAST HOUSE ON THE LEFT, focused on two young bogans who commit a crime, commit more crimes, and then get their just desserts at the hands of a young mob of teens and twenty-year-olds. The hero of the story is a young woman who gets fed-up with the conflict (bogans being bogans), picks up a gun, and aims it her abusive bogan boyfriend, whose sole purpose in life is to get laid, or in Aussie at the time, have a "root."

Bogans are prevalent in Aussie cinemas. They're pretty much every character in Ted Kotcheff's WAKE IN FRIGHT, but street bogans weren't overly well represented in the mid-80s. Our bogans also broke the mould because both of my lead actors were big New Romantic/New Wave fans, as I was too. So, although they spoke like bogans, they looked more like Ultravox with guns, chased by a posse of Human League lookalikes. At the time, Aussie New Wave bands like Pseudo Echo were selling out clubs and re-shaping hairstyles, so it made sense to blend the two cultures rather than insist that my actors get haircuts and remove the eye-liner, which definitely wasn't going to happen.

MARAUDERS, not surprisingly, got slammed by several Aussie critics as it just didn't "represent" how the local film culture wanted the world to see us. That reaction was part of the fun, and it was satisfying seeing a few local stuffed shirts getting all high and mighty over it. Of course, later on, a few bogan masterpieces emerged—Rowan Wood's THE BOYS, in particular, is bogan heaven—and television embraced bogan crime with series like BLUE MURDER and UNDERBELLY. But MARAUDERS, the first ever Aussie feature shot on broadcast video cameras (by Ikegami), went on to sell quite well overseas and it eventually got a legit US release—as opposed to its pirated release—as part of a Savage Sinema box set of my movies.

This novelization you now hold in your hand, courtesy of Sawyer Perry, is a really innovative take on the original material, and I reckon Perry has nailed the Aussie landscape and its bogan culture very deftly. I laughed out loud several times and, even to me, there were a few surprises.

Enjoy.

Mark Savage
Director/Writer
MARAUDERS

MARAUDERS

marauder (*noun*)

    a person or animal that goes from one place to another looking for people to kill or things to steal or destroy

CHAPTER 1
"YOU BETTER WAKE UP, J. MUM'S CALLING THE COPS."

Studies have found there is a correlation between heat and violent crime. Reportedly, violent crime increases by up to 5.7% on days with temperatures higher than 29.4 degrees Celsius (85 degrees Fahrenheit).

World weather maps have fingered Australia as the hottest place on Earth.

These are the kinds of things scientists devote their lives to figuring out.

These are not the kinds of things criminals bother themselves with.

* * *

One nice morning in a nice red brick house with a lemon tree out front (J.D.'s) in a nice city (Melbourne) in a nice country (Australia) on a nice continent (also Australia), a little boy ran down the hallway to wake up his older brother with the seeming enthusiasm of Christmas-morning purpose. He was fresh-faced and impressionable, with a ginger tinge to his hair and a similarly pale orange blood spatter of freckles over his nose and cheeks.

Old people were always telling him he looked like Opie on *The Andy Griffith Show*, but he didn't know what that meant and definitely didn't care enough to look it up. He had enough on his plate.

"You better wake up, J. Mum's calling the cops," he exhaled in one breath in warning as he burst into his older brother's still-dark room, covered in posters for punk and metal bands J.D. didn't even listen to. He just liked how violent their logos and designs always were. His favorite was a drawing of a hand holding a hammer. It was smashing into the red silhouette of a head, blood and gore exploding everywhere. There was a half-drunk bottle of whiskey sitting alone on his nightstand.

Out of the mouths of babes. The thought came to J.D. in his still half-asleep stupor. He remembered his granddad would say that shit every time J.D. cursed as a kid. Which was a lot. J.D.'s granddad died a few years back when he choked on a Tim Tam. A Tim Tam is a chocolate biscuit. It's also a mildly racist but (allegedly) affectionate term for Asian people based on the somewhat dubious stereotype of Asians moving to Australia and piling their grocery carts up with packages of the cookie at Woolies. But it doesn't actually matter what it is, the point is that his granddad's was the kind of death that made even non-sociopaths punch out an involuntary laugh when they heard it. His mother's punched out laugh immediately morphed into a series of hacking sobs that didn't let up for several days. But J.D. just kept on laughing. Craig, J.D.'s little ginger brother, didn't laugh or cry. He just stood there quietly. When you lived with an older brother like J.D., you learned pretty quickly to stay back and stay quiet, not to react to anything too quickly. Like sharing a flat with a beefed-out kangaroo buck.

The rules were pretty similar, in fact. Any expert worth his salt will advise you, in the event of an unexpected encounter with a kangaroo buck, the best course of action would be first to try to remain calm, then to make yourself appear small by keeping low to the ground, to avoid eye contact, and finally, to slowly back away without turning your back on the animal. And for a predator, hunting is an innate behavioral response to the sight of prey. So whatever you do, for fuck's sake, don't run.

It was much the same with J.D.

J.D. pushed up in bed, rubbing at his eyes, already irritated. He was the kind of good-looking (nice face, dark hair that fell naturally in a pleasing way, blue eyes under nice eyebrows) that suggested he didn't truly need to be like this. Like when the odd woman sees a picture of Ted Bundy for the first time and wonders why a nice-looking, handsome guy like him needed to do all that. Couldn't he have just asked the women out? Been nice to them? Bought them dinner? But that's missing the point. It's like when submissive women marry dominant men and then wonder why their husbands hate their guts. Who wants a horse somebody else broke? Or worse, that broke itself? What the hell does that prove?

"What do you mean she's calling the cops?" J.D. replied. As if he didn't know. Playing dumb or being dumb, whichever one it was, he was good at it. It was one of his best party tricks. It was one he employed frequently with his own apex predator, who also happened to be his best and only friend. If you were using the term "friend" liberally.

"Said she's gonna. Said she can't stand the dead bodies no more," Craig went on.

"Figured the bitch wouldn't keep up her side of the bargain," J.D. sneered. "Where is she now?"

"Gone to get some milk."

Gone to get some milk. Sounded like bullshit to J.D. Sounded like the last thing a deadbeat dad says to you before you never see his sorry ass again. "Going out to get some cigarettes." J.D. didn't know what excuse his own dad gave. He was too young to remember. He remembered well what Craig's dad said though. "I'm not spending one more minute in this godforsaken house with your psychopath of a son!" J.D. almost laughed as he recalled it, before remembering he woke up in a bad mood and why. This was about the good-for-nothing parent who stayed.

"Okay then, quick as you can, Craigy. See if you can find us a knife. Gonna have to kill her."

Craig didn't even flinch, bless his little ginger heart. In some ways, J.D. wished Craig would get older quicker. He would be a much better partner-in-crime than his own. J.D. could finally call the shots. Be the one who gave orders.

But deep down, J.D. knew he didn't really want that. He liked not having to call the shots all the time. He liked following and then just doing. Not having to think too much about it. Thinking wasn't the fun part anyhow.

Craig let go of the door and ran off to do as he was bid. Maybe Craig should have cared more. Maybe he should have had more of a reaction to his older brother casually suggesting their mother had to die. But at this age, little boys are like house cats, fiercely certain of their need for independence, to be left alone and let live, and entirely, willfully obstinate to the fact that they'd starve to death in dirty clothes and soiled sheets if it weren't for the complex emotional and physical infrastructure provided largely by their mothers.

But none of that was clear now. All that remained was a simple equation. If J.D. killed their mother, J.D. will be happy, and Craig won't have to do any more chores. Craig wasn't particularly strong in maths, but he could suss out that much.

He went to find a knife.

* * *

J.D.'s mother, Dorothy, was a schoolteacher. She was a good teacher. All her students loved her. Even the misbehaved ones. Sometimes especially the misbehaved ones, as she tended to end up giving them more attention than their more well-behaved counterparts. Wasn't that always the way? The squeakiest wheel always getting the grease? Dorothy's sons might argue their beloved schoolteacher mother paid more attention to her students than she did to her own kids at home. Every once in a while, they saw fit to remind her of this. Or to accuse her of this, which is how it felt to her.

Dorothy would always tell them that, for one, not all of her students had loving parents at home to watch out for them properly, and for two, when Dorothy was at school "spending time" with these kids, she was also at work. Making money. To support her boys at home. To put food on their table and in their ungrateful bellies.

The truth, if Dorothy would allow herself to admit it, was different than that. J.D. was not yet eight when she found him torturing a rabbit in the backyard. When she asked him, horrified, what he was doing, he just smirked at her and told her to pipe down. Then he stood up, brushed off his pants, and asked her what was for dinner. For a moment, he reminded her of his father.

The next time it was a possum.

The next time it was a neighbor's elderly dog. (That was around the time Dorothy stopped eating meat. Though J.D. very much still did, so she still found herself cooking it near daily.)

The next time it was a girl in his Year 10 class. He didn't kill her. But what he did was enough.

By now, he had graduated from school, but not his habit.

There wouldn't be a next time, she was certain of that. The problem now was that she was finally admitting it. That's why she was contacting the cops. She only wondered... She had brought J.D. into this world, would he be the one to bring her out of it? (And is that the reason why she hid all the knives before she left the house early that morning?.)

Either way, she took a deep breath and walked into the police station.

* * *

Craig watched out the front window as his mother approached the house. She didn't have any milk with her.

Craig didn't hesitate to call out to J.D. to let him know the enemy was fast approaching. He didn't even think about it. Maybe it was because he hadn't really had a real father and so in a way J.D. was like his father. And he wanted to please him more than anything. Or maybe it was just as with most humans, and Craig was just as good as any at taking orders no matter how repugnant, as long as they served to save his own hide. At any rate, it wasn't something Craig thought about a lot if at all.

Craig's mother hauled herself up the street toward her house, not knowing what awaited her. She was sporting a relatively fresh haircut (she'd gotten fringe) that she'd spent too much money on, but it had made her feel just a little bit better at the time and therefore had seemed worth it. It didn't really matter either way, as she was currently wearing an outfit only a librarian, a kindergarten teacher, or a nun would put together. (Or some unholy combination of the three.)

She probably didn't think it was that bad herself, but undoubtedly if she had been told it was the outfit she was to die in, she'd have picked something else. Maybe that nice little black number she'd worn to her mother's funeral. It was just a little too short to be appropriate for such an occasion, and it had given her a little thrill at the time. Her mother would have hated it. If she'd been alive, that is.

Craig shouted that the enemy was coming up the driveway now. J.D. shouted back to keep it down. These things needed some finesse, after all.

When she walked through the door, the house was quiet. No one to be seen.

By the time she heard the sudden footsteps, she barely even had time to turn around…

Into the butt of a guitar as her eldest son rammed it down into her skull. It made an awful sound. A tinny bonking. There was something almost dissonantly humorous about it. Like when corpses fart during the decomposition process. Did you know the same gut microbiota that help keep you healthy when you're alive will quite literally start eating your body from the inside out the second you die? There's probably a lesson in there somewhere.

If Craig had been able to find a proper knife in time, it would have sounded a lot worse but perhaps would have been a fair bit quicker.

Do you think if she had a choice, she would have picked which way to go? Please, J.D., if it must be done, do it in the living room with the knife in my little black dress.

* * *

J.D. threw a glass of water on his battered mother, who was currently unconscious and tied to a chair in the living room, now set up for dying. Underneath a criss-crossing of dried blood that covered her face from the beating which was a precursor to the tying-up, she groaned, still out of it. J.D. didn't particularly mind this, as he had some things he wanted to get off his chest without any useless interruptions from whinging women.

Craigy watched from the kitchen doorway, but he wouldn't interrupt. He knew better.

"Listen to me. Listen to me!" J.D. began his impassioned rant. "Why the police? Why do you want to involve them? Shit, Ma. Everything was going great. Why couldn't you keep your side of the bargain? What was so hard about doing that? You had all the money you wanted. Whenever I brought them here I gave you all their money always. I never kept any for myself. All you had to do was let me keep them here. Let me work with them and play with them. Nothing more than that. But no, you had to fuck everything up, Mother. Why'd you have to fuck everything up? Why?"

If she had been conscious, she probably would have been thinking about those girls, all the ones she convinced herself were just J.D.'s girlfriends, that their shouts were merely screams of passion, that the money had come from somewhere else…

Perhaps her face would have contorted in hurt and anger as she shouted at J.D. that her only fault was believing he was someone else, someone better…

But as of now, the only activity on his mother's face came from the blood continuing to drip down it.

CHAPTER 2

"WHAT DO I TELL HER WHEN YOU'RE DEAD, EMILIO?"

In a much less quiet home, Emilio tried to head out, but barely made it three steps down the stairs before his ear bashing wife was on his heels like a dog, barking about "where did he think he was going?"

"Out," he replied. She could test the meter of his tolerance for her by the proliferation (or lack thereof) of syllables. One meant it was on the floor.

"Out where?"

"To find a job," he threw back, not all that convincingly. But still, she got four whole syllables that time.

"Bullshit, Emilio," she replied. "You're going out to get drunk with J.D."

"The fuck I am!"

"Christ, it's not even 9 o'clock, and you're thinking about getting drunk already!"

Now the woman was getting mad about perceived slights she'd made up in her head. Perfect. Bloody bonzer. "What the fuck is it to you?" he replied, hands on his hips in righteously perturbed anger.

Accompanying the crude staccato of their shouting were the

searing backing vocals of an infant as it wailed from some back bedroom.

"It's got plenty to do with me and plenty to do with your daughter. What do I tell her when you're dead, Emilio, and she starts asking where's daddy? What do I tell her then?" More useless imaginings.

Emilio bristled even more at this outburst. First, this infernal nag of a woman, and now he had to answer to a baby too?

"Tell her what you fucking like!" he replied as he shoved the mother of his child away from him. For crying out loud, the baby had like a year or more before it even understood words. He wasn't sure. He never read any of those fucking books. Couldn't be bothered. Didn't even mean to make the thing in the first place. After all, any old whacker could fuck a person into another person. Idiots and dipsticks could accomplish as much. "Get off my case, alright!"

"I'll tell her Daddy was a loser and didn't give a shit, that's what I'll tell her. I'll— I'll tell her the truth." Emilio's wife grinned smugly, as if the truth was a thing that mattered. Emilio couldn't even remember what he'd seen in her. Maybe it was that they basically had the same haircut and when they met in that bar, he was full drunk and thought that it had meant something.

At any rate, she got three fists to the chest and one to the face for that last mouthing off. She didn't say much after that. Just made those sad, little animal noises, like a dog that'd finally been kicked.

Emilio left her crumpled on the ground in the darkened hallway, the baby still crying in the background. Or maybe it had stopped by then, he couldn't be sure. He tended to block that kinda stuff out. It was just extra noise, after all. And it was her job anyway. It had little to do with him. Like when you tune out someone else's phone ringing. What's the point? They're not calling for you anyway.

It was ironic, Emilio thought, as he closed the front door behind him. The thing she said, about "what do I tell the baby when he's dead?" Considering if anyone was in danger, it was her. And also because it's a goddamn baby. Imagine that! The baby learning its first words and them being nagging him just like his mother. Just perfect. Bloody bonzer!

* * *

Emilio got to his car that parked and quickly realized he couldn't find his fucking keys. He slammed a fist down on the top of the green four-door Ford Falcon. Which might have worked if it had been an old television. Fucking perfect. First he had to deal with his wife being on the rag or something and now his keys had gone bloody walkabout. He cursed, stomping back to the front door, but in opening it, he encountered a strange resistance...

His wife was conscious again and pressing her weight on the other side of it to prevent him from getting back in.

Emilio demanded to know where the keys were, what she'd done with them. But the *"bitch!"* on the other side refused to answer. She managed to shut the door on him and lock all three of the locks on it up tight. He heard them slide in one by one.

"Fucking bitch!" he responded, looking around for another way in...

As Emilio hauled himself up a drainage pipe along the side of the brick house, he thought about all the things he hated about her. He hated the way she did her make-up. He hated her hair. (He did not see the irony in this last one.) Hated that it was both shorter and thicker than his. He hated her stupid dangly earrings she always insisted on wearing, even if she wasn't dressed up, that always got caught in his collar or in his own hair whenever he forgot for a second how much he hated her and made the mistake of getting too close.

He threw himself through the first open window he could find. By the time his wife, who was still waiting downstairs warily guarding the front door she had just locked, heard his footsteps and spun around to find him lunging down the stairs at her, it was already too late. Perhaps if she hadn't locked all three of the locks on the front door, she could have made it out quicker. Perhaps if she had still been in the kind of shape she was in before the baby, she could have made a run for it.

But she didn't make it past that pesky third lock. He caught her at the door, flinging the last lock off of it and then her out of it, where she crumpled onto the front stoop. He briefly thought about beating the keys out of her, but the more she yelled that she didn't have them, the angrier he got.

"Talk to me, Emilio," she begged him. "You never tell me anything anymore!"

"Then I'll tell ya," Emilio replied. "It's over!"

He reached under his shirt for the pistol he kept in the back of his jeans. He put it to the temple of the mother of his child.

She had three thoughts simultaneously:

One, she remembered the day she'd first cut her hair, because she had seen Emilio around town before they'd officially met, and she knew how much Emilio prized his own. Even though he looked like a lost member of Flock of Seagulls. And how she'd never said anything. She guessed that was fair, because he never said anything about her new haircut either. She'd gotten it cut even shorter recently. She liked her new hairdo. It made her seem older, she thought. Like someone who should be married with a baby already. Instead of someone whose prefrontal cortex hadn't yet finished fully developing.

Two, she remembered the day she got the third lock put on the door. It was because there had been a woman murdered mere steps from her front door several days prior. She had talked Emilio's ear off about it, how they weren't safe here, in this neighborhood that was clearly going downhill since they'd moved there, how they should move. But he only laughed, muttered something about how that wouldn't help and then refused to speak on it further. The next time he was out getting drunk with J.D., she dipped into her secret emergency funds, the ones she kept rolled up tight with a rubber band in the bottom of her sanitary napkin box where he would never bother to look, and she called a locksmith.

Three, she remembered the day she found out she was pregnant. She remembered thinking she should probably just go down to the clinic, that would be the smart thing to do, but some romantic, hopeful part of her had thought, maybe, just maybe, if he had a baby in his arms... That's what they always say, right? Mothers become mothers the instant they discover they're pregnant, but fathers don't truly become fathers until they hold the baby in their—

And then he pulled the trigger.

And she didn't have any more thoughts.

* * *

"Well, are you gonna give me the keys?" Emilio yelled down at the corpse.

The corpse did not respond.

Emilio leaned down in case she was having trouble hearing him. Louder, he shouted: "Are you gonna give 'em to me or not?"

Nothing at all from the nag now!

Emilio sighed.

Then he straightened. And something jingled in the front pocket of his shirt.

He laughed and unearthed the keys from his shirt pocket.

"Aw, shit. Here they are." He giggled like a schoolgirl as he skipped down the front steps.

"Crikey!" he added good-naturedly as he disappeared around the corner to where his car was waiting.

The engine started up, and Emilio drove off.

On the porch, the corpse of his wife sat quietly, just out of sight from the street, no telling when she'd be found.

Somewhere inside, the baby continued to cry.

Emilio wouldn't think about either of them again.

CHAPTER 3

"YOU HAVEN'T GOT ANOTHER GIRLFRIEND, HAVE YOU?"

Across town, Becky got ready for school, diligently brushing her teeth as she examined herself in the mirror, plainly distressed by the barely noticeable teenage bags under her eyes and the current limpness of her blonde hair. She frowned and started brushing her teeth more furiously. She was trying to play a game with herself where it was because she cared deeply about cleanliness (she had heard it was next to godliness, after all, whatever that meant), but in reality, it wasn't about who might look at her teeth but whose tongue might be sliding across them later.

She blushed even at the thought. She was a good girl, in all the ways that mattered, but she was unfortunately at the age where she wasn't sure if her natural desires made her immoral in some way or just a simple and inherent product of biology.

Also, she wasn't really getting ready for school.

She put her hair back in a french braid, the executing angle of which always made her upper arms ache but the end product was usually worth it. She felt pretty with her hair pulled back from her face like that. Baby hairs in front would decline to be restrained and spring out to frame her face in a way that made her feel like an angel in an old Renaissance painting. A Botticelli. But angels didn't do what she was doing, did they?

Afterward, she examined the effect in the mirror. *Yep, worth it,* she thought, as her arms throbbed.

From the other room, her mother lovingly called out to her to get a move on before she missed the bus. Becky loved her mum, but she was rarely home, even now her mother was in the middle of throwing a fiver on the counter meant for Becky's dinner and heading out the door.

"Are you gonna be home tonight?" Becky called out.

"No," her mother replied, as she usually did. "I don't think so, love."

Her mother had become important at work, to Becky's detriment. Becky's mum was a secretary in a real estate office, and as soon as her boss found out Becky's mother was both beautiful and efficient, he decided he had use for her after hours as well. Becky's mother rarely came home for dinner anymore. Or after.

Becky thought about those *Peanuts* cartoons, about how you never really saw the adults, their faces always off-screen, their voices warped and disembodied. She wondered why that was. Was it because Charlie Brown had a bad relationship with his parents? Or was it because the creator of *Peanuts* did? She used to think it was so funny. The sound the adults made in the cartoon when they talked. Like a broken down trombone. She wasn't so sure it was meant to be funny anymore.

Becky started at the sound of the front door closing, left with the uncomfortably loud silence of her loneliness. And her guilt. She loved her mother. She knew her mother loved her too. But, still, she was *gone*. Like she usually was. Becky wondered what it said about her that she felt guilty for betraying someone she had made up in her mind.

The quiet of Becky's near-empty house was interrupted by the phone ringing. She was expecting her boyfriend, David. It was new, him being her boyfriend officially. She thought maybe he'd ask her to dinner at a nice restaurant, one with cloth napkins and romantic candlelight the like. But instead, he followed it up by coaxing her to skip school so he could show her his family's cabin in the country. He said it was quiet. Not like the bustling, big smoke that was Melbourne. She thought it sounded romantic. Other girls could keep their cloth napkins and sparkling water, she was getting a getaway in the country. It was like a dream.

Well, except for the part where she had to skip school. She never did anything like that before. But no guy had paid attention to her like David had. He was a couple of years older than her. He didn't have to skip class. At any rate, she wasn't going to mention it again to him. She didn't like to remind him she was still in school. Which didn't fully make sense, as she was in her school uniform when they had met. But still, it felt embarrassing somehow. Like she wasn't a full grown-up yet. But she was, she thought. This little outing, this little act of rebellion today proved as much. Everything would be fine, and it would be worth it.

As she answered the ringing phone, the most beautiful sound in the world, she was certain, she breathed out, "David, is that you?"

It was.

He wanted to know if everything was set for today.

She wasted no time confirming it was and that she'd meet him at nine. He tried to get off the phone without saying I love you, but she didn't mind going first if he needed a reminder, if he needed to be prompted like an actor on stage whose next line had simply slipped his mind. If she could skip school and lie to her mother, she could certainly be the script supervisor of their love.

"I love you," she said emphatically into the phone.

"Yeah," his laugh tinnily followed through the earpiece. "Me too."

The dial tone rang out dully, but somehow the silence got louder. In that silence, she replayed the conversation in her mind, going over her cadence, her tone of voice, to make sure she'd kept it cool. She believed she did. Except for the "I love you," perhaps, but he was still spending the day with her, wasn't he? Everything was still fine. Everything would be perfect. Everything would be worth it.

*** * ***

David lounged shirtless in his bedroom across town, smoking a cig. He had no posters on his walls. He had no real interests or hobbies. Well, apart from this. He hung up.

The brunette woman in bed next to David reached over to pluck the cigarette out of his mouth, taking a drag before asking who that was on the phone.

"Just a friend," he replied.

"What kind of friend?" she responded in that overly casual way that only proved to give away how much she truly cared about the response.

"Just a friend, ya know?" he replied, actually casual.

"You haven't got another girlfriend, have you?" she pressed, less casual now.

"'Course I haven't," David smirked. "Why would I?"

"Perhaps this friend's prettier than I am…" she prodded like a bull.

"Oh don't be ridiculous. I thought you trusted me," he swung back.

She curled up to him as close as she could, head tucked under his chin, fingers curling around his sternum.

David thought about his own mother, long dead by suicide, about how he clung to her embarrassingly as a child, always pulling on her skirts, always trying to climb up her torso for a hug, for comfort. She got cancer, inoperable, and started smoking and drinking in earnest. It pissed his father off something terrible. Was this how she wanted to go out? He was always wanting to know, always yelling. And his mother would just laugh and say it was better that she chose. She accused them both of wanting too much from her. Little leech and big leech.

He remembered his father stomping out. And his mother turning to him and smiling this wide, unsettling smile, as she accused him of being a little worm perpetually trying to wriggle his way back up inside her. Well, he could keep trying if he wanted. Maybe if he figured out how to get his little parasitic self back up in there, the cancer could have a little something else to eat on for a bit, to keep her going for a while longer. She started to lift up her skirt... Did he want to try?

David flushed as he remembered tucking tail and running. He hid under his bed until he heard the gunshot. He stayed there until his dad forced him out to get ready for the funeral. By then his stomach was churning, but he couldn't keep anything down for a week. He never told a woman he loved her and meant it again. Neither did his father for that matter. Maybe that's where he learned it from. He couldn't remember. Rather a chicken or the egg situation, eh?

The girl coiled herself even more tightly around David, like a boa constrictor with octopus

legs curling all over him, like suckling tentacles, each one irritatingly oblivious to the train of his thoughts.

On the other side of her, another girl, this one a redhead, yawned as she turned over in bed.

Gun to his head, he could not tell you either of their names.

* * *

Becky didn't have a car, but that was okay. She didn't mind walking. Especially when the destination was so worth it. She was going to meet David. The sun was shining, the birds chirping, and the vegetation all around her so disarmingly green. It was a truly beautiful day. But Becky didn't notice any of that. She always carried an anxiety about her when she wasn't with David. She simply had to suffer through those awful liminal periods between being on the phone with David and being *with* David. It was like hanging suspended in some sort of purgatory in low oxygen, swinging between certainty and complete uncertainty, where everything became a question, where everything was in question.

Like... What did he do when she was not there?

Who was he with?

Who did he think about when she wasn't right in front of him, forcing him to allow her entry to occupy his thoughts?

But it wasn't long until nine o'clock. She just had to keep walking.

Becky stopped to change from her school outfit to something a little more comfortable for the day. The freestanding public restroom she used was known by many in the area as being in the international registry of pedophile pickup joints. But Becky didn't know that. She changed from her school clothes and into a more casual red shirt and white shorts without a hitch. Maybe it was because it wasn't an international pedophile pickup spot after all. Or maybe she just got lucky.

Her clothes were a little oversized and somehow made her look even younger than her school outfit did. Now dressed and ready, she waited dutifully at the designated meeting spot for David. She watched every car that passed by her street corner, eyes boring inside like twin lasers trained to look only for him. Like a Terminator programmed to love.

She was so anxious. She was embarrassed by how anxious she was. But she had never so much as been late for a single class. She had never done this before. She went over the phrase in her mind. It was like when a woman takes a guy back to her place for the first time and often says, like clockwork, "I've never done this before." And "I really never do this." She *had* never done this before. Becky repeated it in her head like a mantra, like a Hail Mary, the adequate repetition of such ensuring her absolving of the very crime.

But as soon as she was with David, everything would be fine. Soon.

CHAPTER 4
"COME ON, BABE. LET'S PARTY."

Nearby, J.D. waited impatiently for Emilio to pick him up. He played the "I see something..." game in his head to pass the time. *I see something yellow,* he thought to himself. He looked around until he spotted a sign posted next to a low clearance bridge off to his left. It read, "Beware of Cars." He grinned. He was winning the game handily.

But soon, he became increasingly bored of looking out for the ugly green car and started passing the time by downing a bottle of port. *Breakfast of champions,* he thought. He wondered what it would taste like soaked into Weetabix.

Probably terrible.

He'd definitely be trying that soon though. Maybe he could quit his life of crime and start a new line of alcoholic cereal. He could find some drunk retired athlete to endorse. Like David Boon. J.D. could just picture the cricketer on the cereal box, his bat in one hand, and a bowl of beer-soaked breakfast cereal in the other, fully pissed.

Finally, Emilio's green Falcon pulled up across the street. J.D. grinned, near-slack-jawed in his joy and inebriation, as he shuffled drunkenly over to his friend's vehicle and to its passenger seat where he belonged.

At the same time, a brown car sped around the corner. J.D. barely had time to react, even if it weren't for the drunken stupor he was currently swimming lazy laps in.

The car didn't even slow down. It hit J.D. in full force, clipping his legs and sending him flying into the air like a drunken figure skater, before slamming him to the ground. The bottle of port he was carrying shattered across the asphalt, composing a shimmery, broken tune in its wake, before it too shattered and split apart in the wind like a dandelion.

Emilio jumped out of the driver's side of his car screaming a soliloquy of obscenities at the unseen driver.

The brown car didn't even slow down. Emilio squinted to try to spot the culprit inside, but before he could make out much of anything, the vehicle sped up, swerving left and disappearing around the corner. But not before a single arm shot out of the driver's side window and flipped them the bird!

Emilio ran to J.D., hauling his friend to his feet. J.D.'s rear flashed a disconcerting red, but it wasn't blood. It was only his underwear showing through his freshly torn jeans like a bright red, poly-blend flag.

Emilio dragged his groaning friend up and into the car so they could give chase.

The little bastard in the brown car better watch out. The only thing worse than a bored psychopath is a psychopath on a mission. And even more so, a psychopath with a point. Considering they'd happily kill people for nothing but a bit of fun, who knew what Mr. Shitty Driver in a Shit-Colored Car was about to have coming to him if they happened to catch up to him…

* * *

Nearby, Becky continued to wait on her designated street corner, her head buried in a book. It was called *The Survivor* by James Herbert. Becky had quickly read the blurb on the jacket and thought it was just about the aftermath of a plane crash. But soon, she would find out it was much worse than that. She liked the part at the beginning, before the crash, where the old man talked about taking a walk outside, looking up at the night sky, and enjoying feeling small in the magnitude of nature around him. There was something comforting about that, she thought. It made her want to rent a boat one weekend and take it out until she could no longer see the shoreline. To sit in the quiet there. With just the birds above her and the fish below. No people anywhere. Nobody to want anything from her. Nobody to not want anything from her.

A brown car finally came to a stop directly in front of where Becky had her head buried in her book.

David leaned his head out the window, eyeing Becky over his sunglasses. "Come on, babe," he said. "Let's party."

Becky looked up from her book, grinning wide, like a little kid who had asked for a baseball bat and then ran down Christmas morning to see wrapping paper in the shape of said bat leaning against the tree.

Becky put her book away. She would find out who the survivor was later.

"Okay," she grinned even wider, the day she'd been looking forward to finally beginning. And perhaps, one could argue, the life she'd been looking forward to finally beginning too. She wasted little time getting in, and the second she slammed the door closed, they sped off.

Not far behind them, a green Falcon followed.

* * *

"Better get in the left lane, mate, you're gonna lose him," J.D. backseat drove from the passenger seat.

"I don't need your input," Emilio retorted on instinct.

"Well, I'm giving it to ya," J.D. insisted.

"Just like you gave it to your mother?"

Emilio and J.D. were not great at conflict.

"Shit, where the fuck's he going?" J.D. put his focus back on a much more important and mutual goal: getting this asshole and beating the living shit out of him.

"Dunno, I'll pull up alongside him and ask him, okay?" Emilio sneered back.

"I told you to get in the left lane!"

"I said I'm not interested in your opinion!"

"Well, I'm giving it to ya!"

"Buzz off!" Emilio's gaze caught the petrol gauge. The little fucking arrow was not leaning in the direction he wanted. "We're gonna have to stop for petrol, mate. I'm running on a rag."

"We're gonna lose those two," J.D. whined. Like a toddler.

"You got some money?"

"Not a cent." Neither would a toddler.

"Let's hope they're big on charity around here," Emilio grinned, his mood again on an upswing at the thought.

This was probably J.D. and Emilio's favorite genre of joke. Or at least the one that made them feel the most clever. It was like a game. This morning, we're going to play the part of a couple of guys who wouldn't kill their own family because they were in a bad mood. And then later this afternoon, we'll play pretend that we're hoping for charity instead of another opportunity to experience the way it feels to sink a knife fully into soft flesh.

They pulled into the next petrol station honking their horn. The attendant, a pretty blonde in jeans and a flannel, strolled up to the car. "Leaded or Unleaded?"

"Just fill it up."

Helpful, she thought. "I'll need the keys."

Emilio tossed them out the window at her, where they fell mockingly at her feet. She looked down at the keys, swallowing a sigh. Her name was Janie. She'd dealt with plenty of guys like them before. If she hadn't been at work, she might've tossed the keys right back in their smarmy faces. But she was at work. And she couldn't be bothered to get fired right now. And she was a woman, after all. She knew better than most that sometimes the easiest way out was through. She'd learned that lesson a million-odd times already in her young life. War might be a man's pastime, but the old saying "pick your battles" was invented for women and girls to survive to the next day.

She leaned down and picked up the keys.

J.D., who made a show of not checking her out the first time he saw her, freely leered at her the second her back was turned to fill up the car.

The pump clicked as it finished its job, and Janie rotely informed them that'll be twenty

bucks.

"Twenty bucks!" Emilio scoffed. "I haven't got twenty bucks. Have you, J.D.?"

"I haven't got twenty bucks," J.D. replied.

"But I've got this!" He added, just before he lunged at her, grabbing the back of her neck to yank her forward into the car. She barely had time to scream before he shoved a pistol in her mouth. Her eyes went glassy as she went into shut-down survival mode.

The easiest way out is through.

"Suck that bitch!"

Pick your battles, Janie.

Emilio's foot stabbed the accelerator to the floor, and they sped off on their newly full gas tank, as Janie's legs flailed uselessly out the window. For miles, her legs kicked out in every direction, futilely trying for purchase they would not find.

When they got far enough away, only thick trees on either side of them, they tossed her out of the car like an old take away bag, and she went rolling off the side of the road.

She didn't get up.

They pulled off, heading back onto the road, realizing they hadn't seen the brown car in some time. But they were determined to find him. Psychopaths on a mission, after all.

They'd already forgotten about her. They shouldn't have.

* * *

They finally caught up with the brown car in the next town, parked innocently in front of a charming little post office on main street. They watched it as they slowly drove by. Nobody inside. Emilio parked his own car in a side alley and popped the trunk.

Emilio grabbed a tire iron.

J.D. grabbed a sledgehammer.

Then they exited the alley and followed their target.

CHAPTER 5
"LAST HOUSE ON THE RIGHT, EH?"

David ushered Becky into a take away joint. (There weren't any cloth napkins, but he still paid.)

And Emilio and J.D. followed them.

David and Becky ate their lunch on a bench in a park nearby. (There wasn't any candlelight, but it was still awfully picturesque. David hardly spoke to her as he scarfed down a bucket of fried chicken thighs a foot away, but she didn't think about that too much. She just ate her sandwich. He did offer her some of his fizzy drink though.)

And Emilio and J.D. followed them.

When David and Becky got back to David's car, they found it completely trashed. Smashed to hell and the paint scratched all along one side. Every last pocket of air had been slashed out of all four tires.

Becky insisted David should call the police, but David didn't seem interested in that idea. He told her they oughta give it a push, and it'd be fine.

Becky peered at him strangely, confused by his odd non-reaction. This hardly looked like an accident to her. It looked more like a message.

Inwardly, David was pissed. Beyond pissed. That kinda angry

you get where you're so mad, you can't even form words anymore and somehow you're coming off as preternaturally calm instead. But he wasn't. He loved this car. It might have been an ugly shade of shit-stain, but he had been gifted the Mazda on his sixteenth birthday by his dad. It was the same car as his dad's too, though a newer model.

Apparently, the name meant "to fly" in Aboriginal, but that could have just been some shit his dad had made up. When he'd passed him over the keys, his dad had whispered in his ear that to fly meant freedom, and to his dad, the cabin was freedom, but he still needed a way to get there, he'd added with a cheeky wink. David's dad was a bit of a pants man, to be honest, but then again, so was David. The car had been a symbol of their connection. Anyway, it was fucked to hell now.

Becky watched anxiously as David tried and failed to fix one of the car's busted tires. David wanted her to keep pushing, but she refused. He huffed. Finally, he told her to wait there and that he'd be back. She even more anxiously watched him head off, not sure what his plan could possibly be now. And very much wondering if whoever had done this to David's car was done leaving their message…

Becky waited for David under a sun-bleached stone statue of a soldier that was slowly being overtaken by some sort of moss. She wasn't sure which war it was for. She thought it was WWI, but the monument wasn't well-marked enough to be sure, which felt like it sort of defeated the purpose in her opinion. She kept waiting. She'd had a lot of practice waiting for David already in their short time knowing each other. She watched as two guys beat up on an unlucky third across the street. She didn't want to get involved, but she couldn't stop watching them.

She thought about those photojournalists who photographed starving children in war-torn countries but declined to help feed them as it broke some journalistic oath she was at the moment forgetting, something about tainting the authenticity of the scene, but then they'd go crazy with guilt after, long after they'd returned home to their cozy, air-conditioned flats, not actually needing a photograph to remember all they saw and all they declined to do.

Finally, a red ute drove up, honking its horn insistently at her.

Becky leaned down to see who was driving (and honking) and was surprised to find David inside.

"David, where'd you get that?" she asked, a curl of unease winding its way through her stomach as she examined the newly acquired Suzuki Mighty Boy David was now beckoning her to hurry up and get in.

"Uh, car rental's up the road…" he lied easily.

"Yeah, but what are you gonna do about the other car?" she readily accepted that falsity if she could sacrifice it to root out some kernel of truth elsewhere.

"Forget it, it's a miss," he replied impatiently. "Come on, we're wasting time. Let's go."

Becky wondered how they could be wasting time if the plan was just to spend the day together, but she didn't see the point in arguing.

As they drove off, Becky didn't notice the guy running after them, pumping his legs furiously and yelling as he watched his car being driven away.

* * *

J.D. and Emilio ran out of Foster's Bottle Shop with a few choice bottles, and old Mr. Layman who ran the joint (and the attached hotel) on their tail, yelling at them to come back.

"I don't think so, bud," Emilio informed the man, rather pleasantly for once. "They're ours now."

He caught up to them at the car. "Look, son, you and your mate owe me 27 dollars," the old man lectured. "I don't know what you're gonna do about it, but I wanna get paid. You just don't steal from hotels, ya know that? I don't know what you are or what you do. But I want you to pay out, get out of town, and I'll forget about the whole thing."

During the whole of the man's smug little speech, Emilio listened enthusiastically, leaning forward and making proper eye contact, while even more enthusiastically miming jerking off one of the stolen bottles of port in his hands. Up and down, up and down, as Emilio smiled and smiled and smiled back. That was the only response the old man would get.

Mr. Layman watched angrily as the two sped off. He didn't realize how he had made out like a bandit. Didn't even get pistol-whipped or anything! What was he whining about anyhow? If the Grim Reaper showed up at your door and said it was time to go except if you handed over a few bottles of port, you would hand them right over, no questions and no whinging.

Yes, you would.

* * *

J.D. took a leak against a tree on the side of the road, his red underwear giving him away like a lit-up marquee amidst the dull, woodsy backdrop. He was as sloppy at pissing as he was at everything else. He shook his wet hands off and found some fallen leaves to wipe the piss off his boots. Then he flung the eucalyptus leaves away and wiped the sticky residue they left on his already wretched jeans. He would've been a great koala, he thought. He used to want to be one when he was really little. Just sitting in a tree, sleeping twenty hours a day, and when he wasn't, eating eucalyptus leaves, getting high, fucking, and getting chlamydia... Well, maybe not the last part. But if he was a koala, that'd only mean there'd probably be a more aggressive koala who ruled the pack and stole all the lady koalas from him and his name would probably be Emilio.

As soon as he got back in the car, Emilio was on his ass again about losing them. He was always on his ass. Aggressive koala motherfucker.

"Admit it was a stupid thing to do," Emilio pressed.

"No, because it wasn't a stupid thing to do," J.D. flung back. What was Emilio even going on about? He was just as excited to stop and rob that bottle-o as J.D. had been.

"Whaddaya mean it wasn't a stupid thing to do? It was, I'll admit that. You won't admit anything."

"Oh, big fucking hero," J.D. replied. "You can at least admit we both lost them."

"It was your idea first. Look at ya. You've been drunk ever since I picked you up this morning. You're a fuckin' asshole. A drunken, fuckin' asshole."

"You shut up."

"You shut up."

J.D. remembered hearing an annoying cunt of a teacher he had back in primary school harping at him about how anger was a sign of emotional immaturity. Probably some bullshit her divorce counselor told her before confirming it was all her husband's fault. He didn't know what that had to do with him. Or why he was suddenly thinking about it now.

"No, you shut up, cunt," J.D. said. "Just start looking for them. They can't have gone far."

"What would you know?" Emilio spat. "You shit me, J, every-thing about you shits me."

Aw, J.D. thought briefly, insanely, it was almost like a love confession. Or the opposite of one. But they do say the opposite of love isn't hate, now don't they? "Why? Cuz I do the same shit and say the same shit as you?" J.D. smirked, pleased at himself for that quick retort.

"No, cuz you're stupid, and you never think about anything," Emilio responded.

"Aw, come on." J.D. didn't have much of a retort for that one.

Emilio eyed J.D., who just stared out the window, refusing to make eye contact. Emilio scoffed and put the car into gear, driving off.

Almost immediately, they were cut off by a red ute. It was a real close one too. The kind that makes your guts jump up into your throat for a second.

"Asshole!" Emilio shouted.

Emilio started to head off, but J.D. was still looking back at the red ute, two brand new creases in his perfect forehead.

"Hey, turn around. Back there," J.D. commanded with a sudden surety. "It's him."

"Where?"

"In the fucking red car."

"What do you mean? The car that just—?"

"Yeah."

Well, holy fucking shit, Emilio thought. Like bloody kismet. And he'd traded in his shit-stain car for a blood-red one. Just like what they were gonna drain outta him when they caught him. Fucking kismet. Only—

"I can't fucking turn!" Emilio realized, pissed at the traffic.

"Well, we're gonna lose him!" J.D. said.

"What's he doing in that?" Emilio yelled. They'd encountered a real wild one, this time. A hit and run driver who's either a rich freak who's got a stable of cars at his command or is also into grand theft auto. What a day!

"I don't know, just concentrate on turning. Didn't I tell you to stay in the right hand lane?" "No, you told me to stay in the left hand, you shithead. Look where that's got us."

J.D. pursed his lips and turned to look out the window. This is what J.D. did when he knew he was wrong. He never said, "Okay, maybe I'm wrong." He just refused to make eye contact until whoever was pissed at him had moved on.

Emilio grumbled at the oncoming traffic until he was finally able to make a u-ey.

But the red ute was already long out of sight.

They saw a boy, he was maybe thirteen, walking down the road by himself and pulled over to ask him if he saw a small, red car go by.

"Who wants to know?" the little ginger shit replied.

"Jesus wants to know, cunt. You seen it or not?"

"Maybe I have," the kid said like he didn't have a care in the fucking world. Well, they'd give him one.

"Yeah, when?"

"About ten minutes ago."

"Which way'd it go?"

"What's in it for me if I tell ya?" the ankle biter actually said to them.

"A longer life," J.D. replied and grabbed the little shit's shirt so he couldn't run off. The kid kinda resembled J.D.'s brother, Craig, but even if J.D. had made that connection, he wasn't sentimental in that way, so it's not like it would have mattered much.

"Let me go, and I'll tell ya exactly where he went," the kid bargained.

"What do you mean exactly?" Emilio piped up. "You know the guy?"

"Sure," the little shit replied. "He comes down here every Monday. And every Monday he's got a new chick. Guy sure loves fucking." The little shit grinned wide.

Out of the mouths of babes, J.D. thought. Suddenly, he wanted a Tim Tam.

"That's obvious. Where is he now?" Emilio prodded.

"Let me go, and I'll tell ya," the kid now repeated like an anxious prayer. Apparently he was starting to understand the score.

"Address first," J.D. commanded. Emilio grinned. At least J.D. seemed to be getting a little bit smarter. Emilio's influence, surely.

"Guy's dad owns a house down this road. Last on the right. Can't miss it. He's got another two back in town. I reckon the old guy's loaded."

"Is that a fact? Last house on the right, eh?"

"Right! Now let me go!" the kid whined.

"J.D., get rid of this fuckwit," Emilio ordered.

It seemed to be a game of chance whether or not getting rid of somebody meant they'd get back up again after. But right now, they were focused on their real target. J.D. shoved the little shit onto the ground, and they sped off toward it.

* * *

Miles back down the road from where they came, there was movement on the side of the road, something rustling in the grass…

It was Janie, the petrol station attendant. She was still alive. And she was *pissed*.

So pissed, she got back up and immediately started walking.

And walking.

And walking. Her gait was determined. She wasn't just going somewhere. She had something to do. The easiest way out might have been through. But she was done picking her battles.

This time, it was war.

CHAPTER 6

"I DON'T KNOW. THEY'RE JUST KIND OF WEIRD UP HERE."

The recently acquired red ute sped along a back road until it came to a cabin in the middle of the woods. It pulled into the carport. David and Becky got out, and she followed him to the front door. David unlocked it and then turned to look down at her pointedly.

"What are you waiting for?" he asked. "A guided tour?"

"I'm waiting for you to go first," she said.

"Ladies first," David grinned as he watched her give in and head inside.

A mere second later… "Enough of the guided tour," his grin morphed into a leer as he followed her in, teeth showing like a hungry wolf as the door shut behind them.

It was quiet out here in the woods. No one was around. Not for miles.

When David invited Becky to have their first real date in a cabin in the woods, she never once thought of the hundreds of horror movies that start out exactly that way. If she had, would she have been better prepared? If she had, would she have come along in the first place? If she had told her mother where she was going, would her mother have advised her against it? Or would she have just laughed and been proud her daughter had finally found herself a boyfriend?

* * *

Inside the cabin, David headed straight to his favorite part of the tour...

He shoved the bedroom door open, and it creaked out of the way, revealing a room with old wallpaper and a single bed with an ugly yellow and black bedspread. Coming up alongside him, Becky peered dispassionately inside.

"And this is the bedroom," David smirked, his small head full of big ideas. "Kind of cozy, yeah?"

But Becky was already walking away.

He found her in the hallway headed back to the kitchen and living area.

"David, do your mum and dad come here very often?" she asked as she leaned against a counter in the kitchen.

"No, not really," he said. "Dad comes up quite a lot by himself, but Mum hates it."

"What?" Becky asked. "She hates him coming up here by himself?"

"No, stupid," he replied. Becky's jaw flexed with disagreement, but he went on. "She hates the place. This town. The people. This house. She can't understand what he sees in it."

There were two lies in this next statement. The first, of course, was that David's real mother was dead. However, his father had wasted almost no time in remarrying. He and his new wife insisted David call her mum, and as by that time, David was as happy as his dad to pretend nothing had ever happened, he readily complied. Besides, his mum abandoned him and his father, why should they not call this woman who chose them wife and mother? David didn't truly love his step-mum, and at the end of the day, neither did his dad, but that was neither here nor there. And David couldn't be bothered with explaining the difference to Becky and getting into all that anyhow.

The second lie was David claiming not to understand what his father saw in this place, when in reality it was the very same reason David was here now. It was the reason Becky was here too, though she didn't fully realize that yet.

She would.

"I can," Becky said.

"Can you? Well, I can't," David said, already bored with this conversation. Not interested in conversation at all.

"Yes, I can. It's nice here. Listen, you can hear the quiet." She paused for a beat, listening. "You can't hear that back in Melbourne."

Becky thought about her mum back in town, about having to go back, having to answer for skipping school, for all of this, what she'd have to pay for the quiet. She didn't want to think about that. Not now. Not yet.

Another thought occurred to her. "Why did you bring me here if you don't like it?"

"I didn't say that," David replied. "I said I didn't understand Dad coming up here all the time."

"Why does your mum hate the people?" Becky pressed.

"I don't know. They're just kind of weird up here."

"What do you mean by weird?"

"How am I supposed to know?" David was getting sick of talking about this. He didn't bring her here to talk, for crying out loud. "They're just weird. I don't know, they stick together. Mum doesn't like that."

"What's she got against people sticking together?" Becky wanted to know. "They sound friendly. Why would she hate that?"

Jesus, she was like a toddler, David thought. He brought her up here to this cabin, all romantic and such, and all she could do was give him the third-degree about useless shit. Why was the sky blue, David? Why can't pigs fly? How come unicorns aren't real? He had a question. Why the fuck did he drive her all the way out here if they weren't gonna fuck? That's what he wanted to know.

"I don't know. Shit, would you quit with the questions? I'm not in the mood for stupid questions."

"They're not stupid," Becky insisted. "I just wanted to know."

"Yeah?" he grinned, turning it on. "Well, I want to know when I'm going to get a kiss." He gave her that smile he pulled out for special occasions. The one that said I really respect you, and I would respect you even more if only you would take your top off. And then your shorts. And then lie down and shut up.

He pushed off the counter he was leaning against and stepped toward her, pelvis first, moving to back her further into the kitchen.

But she angled out of his grip.

"Maybe later," she said, infuriatingly. "Didn't we just get here?"

David's head lolled to the side with the force of his eye roll as he barely managed to stop himself from pouting outright. Suddenly, he felt like the toddler. He wanted to throw a tantrum until she stopped being so stupid. She was so much more work than the other girls he was used to running around with. That's what had compelled him about her.

That's also what he couldn't stand about her.

CHAPTER 7

"I JUST HOPE THESE TWO AREN'T HEADED HER WAY."

Not too far off in the countryside, something was happening. Three figures cut a stark picture against the landscape as they strode along with purpose.

A posse was assembling.

Janie had already recruited two people she knew in town. She wasn't sure if she'd go so far as to call them close or even friends, but she knew them well enough to know they hated jerks and loved to fuck them up. And she knew they had her back. At the end of the day, that's all that really mattered.

They encountered the red headed kid sitting on a fallen log under a tree. The kid didn't look out of place, considering one of the three members of Janie's nascent posse could still easily be called a little girl.

"We're looking for a couple of guys in a green car," Janie nodded. "You seen them?"

"Yeah, I've seen them alright," he confirmed.

Janie talked to the proprietor of Foster's Bottle Shop in the driveway of his home. The second she saw him, she knew he had seen something. He had that shell-shocked look about him like he'd got into a serious fender bender that morning and hadn't quite shaken it off yet. Turned out it was both not as bad and also somehow worse than that.

"Yeah, they came barging in the pub like they owned the bleeding joint. I even asked them real nice to hand back what they'd taken," he told her.

"And?" Janie prompted.

"Buggers call me a rudehead and whizzed off," he said, still baffled by it. It was sort of sweet, Janie thought, how hard it was for this middle-aged man to comprehend the behavior of a couple of young guys. Well, Janie was a young woman, and she unfortunately found nothing baffling nor sweet about it.

"Well, Mr. Layman, they sound like the same guys to me," Janie asserted.

"They sure do," he said, increasingly anxious. "I don't suppose they mentioned to anybody where they were headed?"

"I don't know," she said. "Maybe they did speak to someone, but then again, it's probably better they didn't know, know what I mean?"

"I know exactly what you mean," Mr. Layman replied. "I sent my Christie out about an hour ago on an errand. I'm expecting her back any minute. I just hope these two aren't headed her way."

Poor, sweet Mr. Layman, Janie thought once more, before she turned and headed off.

* * *

Christie, Mr. Layman's daughter, trudged down the muddy side of the road, errand-bound. Her long, curly dark hair bounced lightly as she walked, framing her pale face.

A green car came around the corner ahead of her. It stopped, pulling over just behind her.

It was *the* green car.

But Christie didn't know that. She kept on, barely bothering a glance behind her, focused on her task. She needed to remember the list, because she often forgot something, which irritated her father. Even though he was the most polite man she ever met, she knew him well enough to be able to tell when he was perturbed. But it was okay, because she would remember this time. *Milk, eggs, bread, and a tin of Milo... Milk, eggs, bread, and a tin of Milo*, she repeated her grocery list to herself, the only real thing on her mind.

Until the car started reversing.

She kept walking, keeping her pace. *Just ignore it*, she thought to herself. *Just ignore them, that's all. Keep walking.*

"Whoo!" someone called out of the still-reversing car.

This got her attention. But almost as soon as she glanced behind her, she turned her head back, keeping her eyes to the front. Sometimes, when in a panic, women thought men were T. Rexes. As long as you didn't make eye contact and kept out of the reach of their stubby, little arms, you would be okay, you could sur—

"Hey, pussy!" J.D. popped his head out of the passenger side window as the car rumbled backward alongside Christie's already picking up steps.

"Hey, pussy!" J.D. called again.

Just ignore him, she thought. She kept walking, head down.

"You snob bitch!" J.D. gritted out, grabbing at her despite her adopted tactic.

She just kept walking.

"Wait!" he demanded.

She did not.

"Come on!" J.D. said. "Get in."

"Fuck off!" she finally replied.

"Do ya swallow?" He grabbed at the sleeve of her green jacket. Even the gloves she had on were green. Green, like the car. Green, like she was meant to be with them. For them. And then he yanked on the back of it, hanging on, until she could no longer ignore him.

"Fucking leave me alone!" She hit him. And ran.

"Oh, fuck you, bitch!" J.D. shouted.

She ran faster, a bit awkward in the clunky white boots she was wearing.

"Jesus, *fuck!*" J.D. yelled, frustrated that the car was still creeping in reverse.

Sensing this, Emilio quickly spun the car around.

For a few seconds the sun dipped low behind the trees, and Christie couldn't see inside the car that was quickly gaining on her, and it almost looked like it was the car itself chasing her. Somehow made sentient and angry, thirsty for blood. Like that movie about a killer car. What was that called again...?

The sun reappeared, and again, she saw their grinning, bloodthirsty faces—

Christie turned and darted into the trees at the edge of the road.

They parked the car, and J.D. and Emilio followed on foot, chasing her through the woods.

Christie ran until she was out of breath. She ducked behind a tree to hide and tried to catch it. The trees here were hardly thick enough to conceal her if they found her. She rested her forehead against the trunk of the tree, trying to keep her ragged breath quiet. The woods were too still, too silent. The silence hurt most of all. It wasn't on her side. She suddenly thought about all the times she wanted to murder the kookaburra that lived in the tree outside her bedroom window for making so much goddamn noise at every hour of the day and night. When she was trying to study. When she was trying to sleep.

She would give her left pinky finger for that kookaburra to show up here right now. To be its most obnoxious little self. Even if it did sound creepily like a person laughing. She hated that little black-and-white arsehole. She hated that sound. She always thought there was something sinister about it. But right now, the silence was mocking her more.

Christie got tired of waiting. She rose carefully from her

partially hidden crouch, her legs aching, and started making her way back, out of the woods.

She never made it.

It was Emilio who came first, seemingly out of nowhere. He grabbed her around the shoulders and threw her gleefully to the ground.

She didn't even scream. Who would she scream for? There was nobody out here but her and them.

J.D. ran to catch up. He didn't want to miss any of the fun.

While he waited for his friend to join the fray, Emilio busied himself kicking the girl on the ground. Over and over. Like she was his wife.

And then, surprisingly, he stopped. And turned away.

Christie didn't waste the opportunity. She pulled up to her hands and knees and started crawling painfully away.

Emilio pulled down his fly, opened his pants, and turned around to casually watch her crawl.

As J.D. caught up, he stopped to watch too.

For what felt like the longest time, they just stood there and watched.

Until Christie realized, too late, that she was crawling away from Emilio... and right to J.D.

He grabbed her by the hair and hauled her up easily, her feet dangling an inch off the ground. His hands gripped both sides of her face, forcing her mouth to split out in an awful smile. Near Glaswegian.

The smile on J.D.'s own face was not so forced. It wasn't forced at all.

Emilio picked up a fallen branch and tested its weight, its thickness, in his hands. It would do just fine. He strolled over to his friend, behind the girl he was holding up, and whacked the branch against her back.

Christie fell to the ground, hand to her aching spine. Her mouth was strangely wet. Blood, she realized. Her whole body was aching. She couldn't ignore this.

J.D. grinned at Emilio.

Emilio gathered phlegm in his mouth and spat it on her. Then grinned back at his friend. Emilio laughed, showing teeth, a real smile. And then his lips pursed in palpable anticipation.

They raped her one after the other. J.D. first, while Emilio watched, leg thrust out, arms folded over his chest, smile on his face, pants open.

Christie's hand reached out to grab onto underbrush, but it wasn't enough to get any kind of purchase.

It didn't matter anyway. Emilio saw and casually stepped on her hand until she let go.

Her hand throbbed. But not near as much as it would have if it had been just that. Now, it was just another ache to add to the list.

She tried to think if there was something she could have done. Something different. She could have run the second they started calling out to her on the road. But they had a car and she was on foot. They would have caught her either way.

After J.D., it's Emilio's turn. He really put his back into it, a look of snarling concentration on his face. Unlike J.D., who preferred to look them in the face, Emilio bent her over a fallen log.

If they had known she was the bottle shop owner's daughter, they might have enjoyed it even more.

The whole time, they didn't say one word. Not even to call her a bitch or a cunt. Or to complain she was taking it like a snob.

Afterward, they dragged her through the woods. She wasn't even dead yet, and they were already onto getting rid of the corpse.

Through the fuzz of her mind, Christie distantly felt one of her white boots starting to slip off. Her left one, she thought, but she was trying not to be too aware of her body. She imagined it in her mind, behind her fiercely closed eyes, playing out like a projection on the insides of her eyelids. She imagined it left there like a glass slipper in the grass no prince was coming to retrieve and slide on his princess's foot. There were no happy endings here.

This was the stuff of original fairy tales. Before Disney got their hands on them. This princess was wading out to sea. This princess was stabbing herself between ribs. This princess was becoming the foam in the ocean.

But that wasn't true either. Because even in fairy tale deaths, there's a sort of poetry, isn't there? But there's no poetry to be found here. Just a white boot left behind, like another piece taken from her, chipped away until there was no more. If she was a bottle shop, her shelves were now robbed bare. Distantly, that made her think of something... something she was supposed to do. Something she was supposed to get. A shop... Shelves...

Ah yes, *milk, eggs, bread, and a tin of Milo...*

She didn't forget. Her father would be pleased.

* * *

They only stopped when they came to an old, rusted out car that had been turned onto its back like a tortoise.

They shoved her inside.

Before they headed off, Emilio reached back inside and grabbed the jacket off of her. He took it with him.

CHAPTER 8
"WHAT FUCKING DIFFERENCE WOULD IT MAKE IF YOU HAD A BRAIN OR NOT?"

Not too far away, the posse was growing. There were over a dozen now. There were more men. There were more women too. Even kids. Including the redheaded boy who'd tipped Janie off. The people standing with Janie had little in common. They had different personalities. Different jobs. They even dressed differently. And they had no real stake in this. Not personally at least. They hadn't had the displeasure of encountering the marauders.

So how did that happen that they all found themselves together on this day, all marching toward the same purpose?

Well, it was like David's (step)mum said. The people here were just weird. They stuck together.

Some of them carried random things, a veritable assortment of ad hoc weapons. Someone carried a long stick over their shoulders. Another mysteriously carried two paint cans. The group was quiet as they strode purposefully forward. There wasn't much to say. Only to do. They were the hunters now. And they wouldn't stop until they found their prey.

The posse continued on. They got to a fork in the road and then split up into two groups to cover more ground as they searched for their targets. They spoke as little as possible. Like a quiet plague wafting into town, covering it like a blanket, and then smothering it underneath.

One group found the green Falcon belonging to the marauders. They used a length of rubber tubing to siphon the tank's gas into the paint cans, transforming the getaway car into nothing more than a pretty racing green paperweight.

And then Janie poured the fresh contents of the paint cans that she pumped into the car herself only hours ago all over the car. *That'll be twenty bucks, motherfuckers,* she thought. No, this time, it will be a lot more…

* * *

After dumping the girl, Emilio and J.D. headed back to the car.

And they kept heading to the car…

Eventually, J.D. piped up. "Okay, smartass, which way now?"

"Straight ahead," Emilio barked back, but his tone said he wasn't so sure. Neither was J.D. But Emilio was always quick to come to the conclusion that he had a good idea and a little slower when it came to admitting it was a bad one.

"Look, I'm sure we came that way," J.D. said.

"Well, you thought wrong. Come on!"

"Okay, how come we haven't come to the road yet?" J.D. tried to reason.

"Before we were running. Now, we're walking," Emilio always talked to J.D. like he was a child.

"What fucking difference does that make?"

"What fucking difference would it make if you had a brain or not?" Emilio snapped back.

"I'm not gonna let you get us lost," J.D. insisted. "I'm leading."

"Ok, then fucking lead!" Emilio had all the time in the world for J.D. to prove himself wrong. Just all the time in the world. He would walk these woods all day and night just to prove a point. Especially if the point was that J.D. was the dipstick and he was the smart one. *All day and all night*, Emilio thought to himself…

Emilio was getting annoyed with walking. To entertain himself, he picked up his pace and started stepping on the backs of J.D.'s ankles.

"Quit it!" J.D. spun around, pissed.

"Quit what?" Emilio smirked. Okay, so maybe being the dumb one was kinda fun sometimes.

"Quit fucking walking on my ankles!"

"I'm not!" Emilio had figured out long ago that as long as you came off as angry enough, you would seem right even if you weren't.

"Aw, bullshit, just quit it."

"Why?"

"Don't fucking shit me, Emilio. You know you're doing it, now stop."

"I'll stop it when you find my car, Mr. Navigator."

"Yeah, I'll find it."

"Well, get moving!" Emilio shoved J.D. And then when J.D. turned around, stomped on his ankle again for good measure.

J.D. didn't say anything this time, just sulked away as they headed off again. The only sound in the gentle woods was their boots stomping through it.

"Okay, that's it, I'm not going another step," Emilio screeched as he came to a hard stop. "You've gotten us lost, you stupid shit!"

"Have I?" J.D. answered from up ahead. "Check this out."

"Check what out?" Emilio stomped up to where his friend was standing and saw it.

A car.

But it wasn't his car.

It wasn't just any car either, though that would likely do at this point just to get them the hell out of these seemingly unending woods. They were bloody Kubrickian.

It was the red ute.

"We're gonna go and get him," J.D. declared.

"No, we're not!" Emilio shot back.

"Bullshit!" J.D. had had it. *This* was a good idea. It was the only idea. He was sure of it. He wasted no time swinging on his friend. He clocked Emilio hard on the cheekbone. Emilio went crashing into the dirt and leaves. But he didn't stay down long. He shot back to his feet and returned the favor. Eight times over.

Upon the eighth connection of Emilio's fist with J.D.'s face, J.D. flew back onto the ground. Emilio lunged for him again, but J.D. lashed out, kicking up and clocking Emilio good on the chin and sending his friend crashing groundward.

J.D. got to his feet. "Get up!" he screamed at his friend who was now the one down in the dirt.

Emilio got up.

J.D. hit him again.

This time, when Emilio got up, he kept punching J.D. over and over and over.

CHAPTER 9

"WHAT'S THE MATTER, BECKY?
YOU'RE GLAD YOU CAME,
AREN'T YOU?"

Back at the cabin, David poured Becky a glass of sherry. He figured it sounded girly enough for her to want to try it. And it would take less time than beer. She took the glass but just twisted the stem in a circle on the countertop, frustratingly not making any move to bring it to her lips.

"Well, aren't you gonna try it?" That was good, David thought. He'd managed to keep his tone real friendly and casual.

"I've never tried alcohol before," she told him.

"Aw, come on," David urged, thinking excitedly about how her tolerance would be shit then, she'd only need half a glass. "Loosen up."

But she didn't. David shook his head and lifted his own glass to his mouth.

"It's good. Try it." There was a smile on his face, but his eyes were big and unblinking as he stared at her, trying to seduce her into his horny vampiric thrall.

He sighed and came around the counter to stand next to her. "What's the matter, Becky?" he asked, moping. "You're glad you came, aren't you?"

"I think so," she said, staring at the countertop.

"What do you mean, I think so?" David pressed, his voice

getting higher. There went that cool, casual tone. "Are you or not?"

"If Mum doesn't find out."

"She won't." *For Chrissakes, were they really talking about her mother right now?* "We're miles from Melbourne. How could she possibly find out?"

"I haven't lied to her before," Becky said. "Not before I met you anyway."

"Well, thanks," David petulantly replied. "Now you're sounding like her." David had never met Becky's mum, but like that mattered. He knew well enough to know most girls didn't want to be compared to their mums.

"I am not!" Becky exclaimed. It was the most enthusiasm she'd displayed since she got in his car. Crikey, what was it about girls and their mothers anyway? No matter how close they are, the idea that they're turning into them is always a horror.

"I get along well with Mum," Becky continued. "I just don't like lying to her."

"Don't be stupid," he said.

"Don't call me stupid!" Becky was keyed up now. "Telling the truth's stupid, is it? Am I stupid to think that you're an okay guy? When all my friends keep telling me what a shit you are? Am I stupid not to believe that?"

"No, you're just worrying too much," David replied, silently cursing out her stupid friends. He didn't really know them either, but they sounded like cunts. "I hate it when you worry."

She softened a bit at that. "I worry, I know. But I'm not stupid! Don't call me that, ever."

He didn't know why she was so sore about that. Was she failing her classes or something? Either way, she seemed real mad. And that didn't really benefit him, did it?

"Sorry," David mumbled, mildly cowed for once. "Truce?"

"Okay."

David grinned. He came up behind her, putting his arms around her, and started kissing her neck.

She quickly shoved him off. "Don't!"

"Don't what?"

"I don't want you touching me," she said in an all too definitive way that he did not like one bit.

"What's wrong with you?" he didn't have to fake this one, he genuinely wanted to know at this point.

"What's wrong with me?" she asked. "What's wrong with you?"

"There's nothing wrong with me."

"Well then leave me alone," Becky said. "I just don't want you touching me. It doesn't feel right."

"When are you going to feel right?" David demanded. "In a couple of minutes? In a couple of hours? Tomorrow? Ever?" He was already on stage three of his sexual rejection-induced grief: bargaining.

"I don't know, David. Just leave me alone!" When Becky turned back around, David had already unbuttoned his shirt. "No!" she insisted, instinctively backing up. "I'm not taking anything off."

"Come on, relax," David coaxed, though his voice was a little too high to be calming.

"David, what's wrong with you?" Becky cried. "Why are you doing this?"

"Why am I doing what?" he asked even as he was reaching for the button on his jeans.

"Oh, come on, why are you trying to—? " She could barely get it out. "Trying to—?"

"Fuck you?" he finished, grinning.

"David!"

"Why am I trying to fuck you?" David continued. "I spent close to $500 on you, Becky. I bring you up here for the day... You *act* like you want me to fuck you."

Becky listened to his little speech, swallowing, her throat bobbing anxiously. She quickly ran through the day's events in her head: every comment, every look she gave. Was she? Was she acting like she wanted to fuck him?

"Why the hell shouldn't I fuck you?"

"Because I didn't come up here to have sex with you!" she said. "I don't care about sex. I just like being with you."

"Oh, 'being with me'? Bullshit!" David scoffed, hand on his hip. "I don't fucking believe that."

"Why not?" Becky cried. "You think just because I'm a woman and you're a man that I came here to have sex with you? You only think of a man and a woman doing one thing together, don't you? Fucking!"

"Oh, shut up before I snap, yeah?" David sniped.

"I came here because I trusted you," she bit out. Why was she embarrassed? He was the one who should be embarrassed. "I came here to be alone with you, yes. But to let you have sex with me... no!"

David angled subtly towards her.

"This is crazy, David," she near-wailed, full of frustration and disappointment: both in him and the heavier kind, in herself. "Stop moving towards me, David!" Becky cried.

But he didn't.

"Stop it!"

He raised his arm and slapped her across the right cheek. Hard.

That was it. "God, David, I'm going home!" Becky said, eyebrows firmly knitted together. "Take me home! I'm not staying here with you!"

"Take yourself home," David muttered.

"I will," she insisted, jaw set.

He grabbed her elbow and yanked her closer. "Just remember, that car doesn't start without me."

"David, please..." she begged.

"*David, please,*" he mocked her. "Take your clothes off, and I'll take you home."

She was suddenly furious. More furious than she'd ever been in her relatively short life.

"You bastard!" she shoved him as hard as she could. So hard it made a smacking sound as his spine hit the counter behind him.

"You bitch!" He lunged at her, but she hit him across the side of his head. As he stumbled and fell on the ground, she ran toward the door, throwing it open and darting out like a rabbit that just miraculously managed to get free from the rabid jaws of a dingo. She wasn't looking back. There was no point. There was nothing behind her that was worth it.

As she ran through the woods, Becky pulled up short when she spotted two guys scuffling through the trees. Her brow furrowed, confused. She didn't think there was anyone out here for a mile at least. What could they be doing here?

David ran up behind her, catching up. He stuck his hands in his pockets in what he'd hoped was an apologetic posture. "Sorry, Becky. I'm really sorry. I'm such an asshole."

But Becky wasn't paying attention to him. "David, what do you think's going on over there?"

"Over where?"

She pointed through the trees at the guys fighting hard. David's eyes widened as he realized who they were.

"Come on," he said, jaw clenching with a combination of anger and anxiety.

"David, what's wrong?"

"Please, Becky, let's go," David begged. He never begged. It only served to make her more suspicious. And more vindicated in said suspicions. Especially the ones she'd accumulated just today. What if some of those things she was trying so hard to explain away as intrusive thoughts were actually just intuition?

"David, who are they?" Becky pressed.

"Later," he said, grabbing her shoulders to try to coax her to come with him. "Come on."

"No," she insisted, shrugging him off of her. "I want you to tell me what's going on. I'm not going back there. Who are those guys?"

"Start walking, and I'll tell ya," he said, trying to adopt an agreeable tone. But he couldn't manage to maintain it for more than a second. Not in these circumstances apparently. "I said walk!" he barked suddenly.

But she only looked back at the two guys fighting again. "No, tell me!"

He grabbed her arm and yanked her in the other direction. "I said walk!"

Becky dragged her feet. "Stop it! I don't want to go back to the house."

"Keep going," he stared at her, eyes frantic, like it really was more of a plea this time than a demand. "Don't fucking argue."

"Who are they?"

"They're trouble, okay?" he said. "Maybe big trouble."

This time, when he pulled her along, she reluctantly came with him.

* * *

Emilio didn't stop beating on J.D. until he didn't get back up. By now, J.D.'s torn pants had also taken a real beating, and the ass of them was hanging on by a thread.

"We wait, okay!" Emilio declared.

"Okay," J.D. managed before collapsing back onto the ground. He supposed he could use the recovery time after all.

Now that J.D. was in agreement, most of the fight went out of Emilio. Emilio sighed and helped his friend to his feet.

* * *

Becky waited in the kitchen, a veritable safe zone compared to the bedroom. Or so she thought.

Her eyes widened as David came out of one of the back rooms carrying—no, *wielding* a shotgun.

"What are you going to do with that?" Becky gasped.

"What's it fucking look like?" David responded. "I'm gonna get rid of those two, aren't I?"

"What?" Becky breathed in disbelief. "With that? You can't just shoot them!"

"Can't I?" David challenged. "Watch me."

* * *

Emilio and J.D. took their time stealthily creeping up to the car and the small cabin. They quietly made their way to the front door. As J.D. waited, Emilio tried the doorknob. It was locked. He put his ear to the door, listening for any movement inside.

Neither of them noticed David and Becky silently stepping up behind them.

"Okay, scumbags! Stop right there."

They both turned at the same time to find David pointing a shotgun at them.

"Well, fuck me dead," Emilio exclaimed. "Just the man we're after." Emilio eyed Becky hovering behind her boyfriend. "And his cum-catcher."

"Shut up!" David spat. Maybe when this was all over and he'd chased these little fucks off like a man, he could spin this all as him sticking up for Becky. He could still get a roll in the hay yet.

J.D. grinned like a schoolboy. It was always more fun when Emilio's attention was on somebody else. Especially when he was in a bad mood. Now everything would be okay again. Now they'd be having fun again.

"What's your name, babe?" Emilio addressed Becky jeeringly.

"I told you to shut up, scumbag!" David said.

"Don't you tell him to shut up," J.D. said. "He'll knock your fucking teeth in."

"I doubt that," David spat, his eyes wide and mouth curled up in a snarl. Becky watched David anxiously. "Look, you two, you're trespassing on private property. And I'm not about to ask you to leave. I'm bloody well tellin' ya!"

"Is that right?" Emilio countered. "Well, what about the apology you owe my buddy here?"

"For what?" David scoffed.

"You know 'for what'! Should I jog your memory? You don't look too smart."

Yes, this was the natural order of things, J.D. thought. Emilio was back to calling assholes other than him stupid.

Emilio shoved his hand out, "Name's Ted."

Likely story, David thought to himself. "Well, *Ted*, I hear one more peep out of you, I'll blow your brains straight back to Melbourne. I'm sick of hearing your bullshit. I want you to get off my property."

"You mean your daddy's property," J.D. butted in.

"Whatever," David said. "Just get the fuck out of here."

"Where's your apology, huh?" Emilio persisted. "My mate Harry here ain't leaving without an apology from ya."

"Well, *Harry*," David said to J.D. "Unless you wanna help your friend take ya to heaven, I suggest you start making some tracks."

"Wait a minute," Becky piped in finally. "What are you two on David to apologize for? What's he done to you?"

"Becky, you keep out of this," David snapped.

"No, I won't," she said. "I want to know what's going on. What is going on?"

"Nothing!' David insisted. Considering the Mexican stand-off they were currently in, it wasn't a very compelling argument.

"Bullshit," J.D. said.

"I told you, mate," David said. "Shut up or I squeeze. Simple as that. Becky, these two assholes are just plain crazy. Cant you fucking see that?"

"But why would they—?"

"I don't know," David cut her off. "Just shut up. All right?" So much for the "gentlemanly defending her honor" spin.

"Hey, bitch," Emilio said. "That macho shit make you hot?'

"You don't get moving in ten seconds, I swear to Lord Jesus, I start shooting," David shouted. But nobody moved. Emilio just stared at Becky, refusing to break eye contact.

"One!" David said. "Two!"

On three, Emilio finally started backing up, J.D. took the hint and backed up too.

"Four!"

J.D. pointed an accusatory finger at David, "Not over yet, cunt!" he promised.

"Seven!" David continued. "Eight! Nine! And hey, if either of you so much as set one foot on this property again, I won't hesitate to kill ya."

David pointed the gun at the retreating marauders until they were out of sight. Then he raised the shotgun up to his shoulder triumphantly.

"Who are they?" Becky asked. "You lie to me, and I'm walking home."

"They're assholes," David said. "Forget 'em."

"How can I forget them?" Becky stood in disbelief, at both the situation as a whole and even more so at David for not understanding how they'd clearly crossed the 'just trust me, okay?' line a good long ways back. "You just threatened to kill them. I'm not stupid enough to believe nothing's going on. I'm probably a lot smarter than the others."

"What others?" David asked.

"There've been others, haven't there? I'm not the first, am I?" Becky asked in that way that wasn't asking.

"Of course you are," David was a terrible liar. Or maybe his heart just wasn't in it anymore. It had been a long day, he was tired, and lying took energy after all, didn't it?

"I don't believe you," Becky said. "Why do you look at me as if I was just another girlfriend of yours?"

"Honestly, I don't know," he said. She couldn't believe it. That was seriously the best he could do? After all of this?

"Then I'm leaving! I can't stand being here. Not when I know something's going on."

She walked away, but not before giving him one last look of disgust and disappointment. That's what really pissed him off. He gritted his teeth and cocked the gun, loading a bullet in the chamber.

She spun around at the sound, her eyes locking on the barrel of the gun currently pointed at her. "Are you out of your mind?" she asked (in that way that wasn't asking).

He kept the gun trained right on her. "You're staying right here, okay?"

"No!" she yelled back. Maybe she should have been more frightened, but at this point, she was just pissed off.

"Yes," he insisted. "And I'm getting a kiss. And maybe more."

"You're not touching me," she declared definitively.

"Says who?" he replied, tightening his grip on the gun. "You ain't got a say no more."

CHAPTER 10

"WHEN IT GETS DARK, WE'LL
GO UP TO THE HOUSE AND
GET DILDOHEAD'S GUN"

Emilio and J.D. made it back to the car, but it wouldn't start. The petrol was inexplicably on Empty. Emilio kept stubbornly turning the key over and over, until the sound of the engine flooding overrode every other sound within range, every bug squeaking and every bug chirping, in the area.

"Shit!" Emilio cursed. "You haven't seen anyone, have you?"

"Like who?"

"Anyone!" Goddamn J.D. was a fucking idiot.

"No…" J.D. replied stupidly.

"Some cunt's been here, haven't they?"

J.D couldn't argue with that. "You don't think that asshole's siphoned the tank?"

"No, I reckon someone's else has been here," Emilio's brain whirred through its mental rolodex of enemies they've likely accumulated throughout their many exploits, much less all the ones from just recently.

"Who?" J.D. asked.

"I don't know," Emilio said. "Someone that doesn't want us leaving here…"

"Well, why don't we siphon shithead's petrol?"

"Yeah," Emilio replied. "Aren't you forgetting what we came back here for?"

"No," J.D. said. He ducked down to search under his seat.

"Good. Once we kill those two, we'll get everything we can from up there, including the petrol."

"Shit!"

"What's wrong?"

"I can't find the gun!" J.D. wailed in disbelief.

"What do you mean you can't find it?" Emilio prodded. "Isn't it under the seat?"

"I left it there," J.D. insisted. "But it's not there now!"

"Are you sure?"

"Look, don't ask me that," J.D. begged. "Of course I'm sure."

"Fuck!"

"Well, don't blame me!" J.D. cried as if already hit. "It's not my fault."

"I'm not blaming you," Emilio said. J.D. wondered if he'd heard him right at first. Because historically, this was not the case. "I just want to know what the hell is going on here. First, someone siphons the petrol, throws it all over the car. Now it looks like someone's broken in and found the gun."

But J.D. wasn't listening anymore. Something had caught his eye outside to their left. "Check this out..."

Emilio peered out the driver's side window. There was a little girl in a Mickey Mouse sweatshirt just standing there, staring at them, her hands behind her back, looking like she just stole something out of the cookie jar and ruined her dinner.

She continued to stare at them, unblinking, like one of those little twin freaks from *The Shining*. Just staring and staring.

And then slowly, almost cutely, she moved her hands to the front, revealing in one of them, she held their gun.

"Shit!" J.D. shouted. "She's got a gun!"

J.D. and Emilio quickly ducked out of sight.

Outside, the little girl crouched in kind, her eyes still glued to them.

After a second, Emilio prodded J.D. "You wanna take a look?"

"No, not really."

"Go on," Emilio forced him up. "Just a quick one."

"Shit!" was J.D.'s report.

"She's still there?" Emilio asked. "She's still got the gun?"

"Yeah," J.D. replied, his curiosity overruling his fear for the moment as he peered at the little girl. "She's doing something though..."

"What?"

There was something in the little girl's other hand, but J.D. couldn't quite see... "Hang on..."

And then he did.

It was a lighter.

She flicked it on, heading for the trail of petrol that led... straight to the car they were currently hiding in.

"Fuck!" was all J.D. could manage to get out as she flipped the lighter on and set the line of petrol ablaze...

J.D. shoved his door open, Emilio only a split second behind him, as the little girl ran off, quickly disappearing into the trees. J.D. frantically stomped out the encroaching fire just before it reached the car.

"What was that all about?" Emilio yelled.

"That little bitch almost blew up the car with us in it," J.D. yelled back.

Emilio cursed. "Which way did she go?"

J.D. pointed off into the woods.

"Let's find the little bitch," Emilio raged. The fire now out and the useless, petrol-less car safe, the two of them ran off after her.

After a minute of catching up, they spotted her fairly easily, her white Mickey Mouse sweatshirt standing out in the brush. They lost sight of her briefly, but they weren't worried. She wasn't going to get away from them now. They turned a corner around a thicker copse of trees and then—*BAM!*

A guy appeared suddenly in their path. He was a big guy. It

only took him one punch to send them both crashing to the ground.

As J.D. groaned and rolled over, his underwear was now entirely on display, the ass of his jeans completely torn open.

The big guy stared down at them both dispassionately.

Emilio reared up, eyes full of fire, but the big guy stood his ground, his fists clenched. Emilio and J.D. turned and ran.

They ran until they got to a shed. Fortunately, it was unlocked. Emilio checked inside.

"You see it?" J.D. asked.

"Shut up and keep a lookout," Emilio said.

"Just hurry up!" J.D. was anxious. He was no fun when he was anxious.

"I said shut up!" Neither was Emilio.

Emilio exhaled when he found a can of petrol. "Looks like we're in luck." Emilio headed out of the shed where J.D. was waiting impatiently, pacing like a lion. Or maybe more like a lion cub. "Let's get out of here," Emilio hissed. J.D. couldn't agree more. They headed back to their car, keeping low in the under-brush, letting it conceal them as best it could.

J.D. remembered a trip they took to visit his granddad when he was little. He wasn't even sure Craig was born yet. He couldn't remember. His granddad insisted on going to the Western Australian Museum in Perth. If there was one universal truth about grandfathers, it was that they fucking loved war. Loved talking about it, loved thinking about it, loved weeping at docu-mentaries and blockbuster movies about it. The ones who had never been to war, they always cried and carried on the most. Anyway, there was this exhibit about guerrilla fighters in WWII, he thought it was. J.D. still remembered their slogan or mantra or whatever they called it: "Hit, hit hard, and run."

He liked that.

When they got back in sight of the car, Emilio ducked, hissing his displeasure. Both the hood and boot were open, and there were two guys messing around the vehicle.

"Who the fuck are all these people?" Emilio said.

"Maybe they're cuntface's friends," J.D. offered.

"Well, they're certainly not my friends," Emilio said.

Of course they weren't, J.D. thought. Emilio had only ever had one friend. Him. "What are we gonna do?" J.D. asked.

"We wait here until it gets dark," Emilio reasoned.

"What for?" J.D whined.

"When it gets dark, we'll go up to the house and get dildo-head's gun."

"Let's fucking go now!"

"No," Emilio said. "We wait. No one will recognize us then."

"I'm not waiting half the fucking night!" J.D. cried. Like he had anything better to do. He didn't have any other friends either. But he was a simpler creature than that. And in truth, he had simpler reasoning: "I'm already freezing my balls off."

"We wait!" Emilio said with a finality. "Okay?"

J.D. huffed. "Okay."

So they waited.

* * *

In the woods, not too far off from where J.D. and Emilio waited, the posse was also waiting.

And growing.

Two guys came and joined the group congregating around a campfire, sitting by Janie.

"Hey Janie," the one on the left greeted her. She gave him a nod in return. "This is Mickey Layman." Janie eyed the serious-looking guy next to him. "HIs sister didn't come home today."

"Hi," Janie greeted him, realizing there was also a palpable sadness in his eyes. He was a sturdy guy, good-looking, looked like he should be taking a break from playing cricket and taking his cheerleader girlfriend on a date. Not here. Not this.

"Hi," he responded wearily.

"How's your dad?" she asked. They might not all have known

each other before this, but they all knew his dad. Mr. Layman was a nice guy. Always charged fair prices at his businesses and always greeted everyone with a smile. She didn't know Mickey as well, but it seemed like smiling was his natural state too. Was.

"I don't know," his expression pulled into a pained grimace. "He reckons those guys got her. He's been sitting on the porch since lunchtime watching the streets for her."

"And what do you think?" Janie asked.

"I don't know," he said again. "I reckon she's hiding somewhere, lying low. She's not stupid, though. She's no wimp either."

"Don't worry, buddy," another guy patted him on the knee in support. "We'll find her."

"Well, that's what I'm here for," Mickey asserted, snapping a bit, belying the deep fear needling him, causing a quiet pall to wash over the group.

The moon was beautiful tonight. Full and bright, low and rust-colored. The color of their campfire. From far away, the campfire gathering might have looked like a real bush telly party, teenagers enjoying their youth, but in reality, it was more akin to a funeral. Had more in common with a wake.

Still, the moon sure looked beautiful. And somehow, its odd color felt more like some auspicious sign than an omen. A harvest moon. What did harvest mean, anyway? To gather a crop. To hunt, catch, or kill any manner of animal for human use or sport.

Mickey looked around the group of mostly ragtag teens and kids, several carrying pitchforks and hoes, and he hoped that was true. He hoped that in the morning they would have a bountiful harvest.

CHAPTER 11

"THE WOODS ARE ALIVE, AND YOU BET YOUR FUCKING ASSES THAT THEM WEIRDOS AREN'T OUT THERE GETTING SUNTANS!"

"Move! Fucking move!" David shouted as he chased Becky deeper into the cabin, holding the shotgun on her all the while. She ran until she hit a literal brick wall, bracing herself back against it as she faced him.

"Look, babe," David told her. "It's me or this. And I'm not talking about shooting you with it. Not yet, anyway."

"David, please," Becky said. "I can't. I don't want to. I'm afraid!"

"Becky, if you don't drop your panties right here and now, I'm afraid I'm going to mess up your face with it. Now, do it!"

"But, David—"

"Do it!" he commanded.

"David, I can't do it!" she cried.

"You fuckin' undress or I'll do it for ya!"

"No!"

"Jesus Christ!" He grabbed her, throwing her against the counter. She tripped, her head smacking against the edge of the countertop. She fell back onto the tile floor, holding her smarting forehead.

David watched comfortably from the doorway down at her. She looked down for the count.

It hurt, sure. But she was only feigning how much. Becky was made of stronger stuff than that. She might not have known that before, but she sure did now. The second her vision

cleared, she got up and ran. She ran around the corner toward the front door…

David followed casually, calmly, like a boogeyman in a slasher film. Like Michael Myers himself, with his dad's old shotgun in place of a glinting kitchen knife. He listened for the sound of the front door opening as she bolted. But there was no sound. As he turned the corner, he found—

Emilio and J.D. And they had Becky captive, J.D. had a fist in her hair and a knife to her throat.

"One stupid mistake, and she's dead," Emilio shouted. "You got that?"

David almost smiled. This is what he was waiting for. There might have been two of them to his one. But he was still the one with the gun.

"I said you got that?" Emilio shouted again.

"Yeah, alright," David said.

"Hey, tough guy," Becky addressed Emilio bravely, the bitterness palpable in her tone. "What makes you think he cares whether I die or not? I'm telling you now he doesn't."

"Becky, shut up!" David yelled. How dare this little bitch! Right this minute, she was glaring at him with the same amount of disgust as she gave the two of them. Hell, *more*. As if he wasn't just as bad but worse as them!

"Hey!" Emilio said. "How about a bit of equal time for the lady?"

"Yeah," said J.D. "Let her talk."

Suddenly, they were feminists.

"Cuntface!" J.D. added.

"You got a move to make, you better make it," Becky advised Emilio. "I can tell he's just about ready to squeeze. As far as he's concerned, nothing stands between that barrel and your empty heads."

David actually looked concerned now. Becky was over there riling them up! He coulda sworn he saw the one with the Flock of Seagulls hair give her a begrudging look of respect for her outburst. How had this all happened? How had it all gone this way?

"Watch your mouth, bitch!" J.D. pulled on her hair, yanking her head back. The knife scraped against the taut flesh of her neck.

"No," Emilio said. "It's okay, J. She's right. Kinda. And she forgets one thing. Casanova here puts his balls before his brains. He's not gonna squeeze anything but her little titties. Well, not before he breaks her little cherry."

J.D. laughed at this assessment, and at David's increasingly sour face.

Becky ground her jaw. That was it. As J.D. was distracted, Becky bit into his hand, the one holding the knife. He shouted, dropping the knife, and she wrangled out of his grasp. There weren't many good options for where to run. She bet on David being the lesser of the evils and angled towards him.

Unfortunately for her, the first thing David did with her now free was to herd them all toward the back room with the shotgun.

"One stupid mistake, and you're both dead," David threatened Emilio and J.D. "Now get in there! Go on!"

"And you..." David grabbed Becky and shoved her after them, "can get in there with 'em!"

"Hey, pal," Emilio shouted at David. "Before you start acting irresponsible with that thing, maybe you should work out what you're going to do with them weirdos you got running around out there. Gonna be a hero all by yourself, scumbag?"

"What are you talking about?" David spat.

"I'm talking about a whole bunch of psychos you got running around in the woods out there," Emilio continued, raising his voice further.

"Don't think for one minute I'm going to believe that sort of bullshit," David scoffed. "I sure ain't as stupid as you and your buddy here. And hell can freeze over before I start striking bargains with you. You got that?"

"David," Becky said, "maybe there's some truth in what they're saying."

"Fucking A!" J.D. said.

"Yeah, and maybe you just proved you're as stupid as they are," David countered.

"Yeah, well, that weren't no guys that almost killed us in the woods just before," J.D. said, still creeped out by the sight of that Mickey Mouse little bitch almost blowing them up good.

"No," Emilio added. "Way more like fucking King Kong!"

"And there's more of them," J.D. insisted. "I saw them! Running around like rabbits and just as fast. Only thing is they weren't scared of nothing."

"You know what I reckon?" Emilio said, staring daggers at David.

"I don't know nor care," David said.

"Shit, I reckon they're watching us. They're out there right now. And if it's the bad guys they're after, they'll be coming in. I don't reckon they're going to knock first," Emilio grinned. He was having fun now. He would really pat himself on the back later for that King Kong line. Fuck, he was funny under pressure. This was the most fun he'd had in ages. Maybe ever. What a day!

"I don't know what the fuck you're talking about," David replied. "Whatever it is, it's bullshit, and I don't want to hear any more."

"Look, you stupid motherfucker," Emilio sneered. "You better start listening to what I'm saying. There's this big dude. A real fucking monster. I don't know how many others there are out there like him. Maybe they're waiting for it to get really light before they make their move. Or maybe they're going to let us sweat it out 'til morning. But whatever they're doing, it scares the living shit out of me."

Jesus Fucking Christ, he was a goddamn thespian. He coulda snagged an AACTA for this performance. Maybe even a bloody

Oscar. He knew they appreciated violence and bullshit over in the States too. Maybe even more so.

"David, do you know who they are?" Becky asked, with a sincerity and a calmness he was honestly fucking pissed she was able to maintain. He was more pissed to admit he was getting more riled up than all of them combined. "Do you know what they could want?"

David pursed his lips, but entertained her enough to check out the window, or at least to put on a show that he was. "I don't see anything," he concluded all too quickly. "And I still think it's bullshit. Anyway, I don't know what the fuck I'm doing listening to your crap."

"Then you're a fucking dead man, jerk!" Emilio berated him. "You kill us, then you're most definitely dead. Am I getting through to you, *Dave?*" Emilio sneered his name mockingly. "The woods are alive, and you bet your fucking asses that them weirdos aren't out there getting suntans!"

"David, maybe they're right," Becky said. "Maybe there is a danger."

She was right. Outside, a lone member of the posse, who continued to wear his sunglasses despite the setting sun, watched them through the window. And waited.

"Dickbrain," Emilio addressed David again by his proper name. As far as he was concerned it was the name that properly suited him best. "She's a hell of a lot smarter than you are, it seems."

"Shut up!" David retorted oh so cleverly. He turned to Becky, gesturing harshly with the barrel of the shotgun. "And you! You can shut up or start taking your clothes off. It's your choice."

"Jesus Christ," Emilio said. "Does that kind of chat turn all the girls on?"

"Not as much as sucking your mother's nipples turns me on, moron," David flared his nostrils at Emilio.

But Emilio wasn't scared. Not in the least. Not of this asshole. He was all talk. Standing there cradling his daddy's shotgun like a teddy bear to make himself feel better. What a fucking dick-for-brains. Besides, there was only one of him, whereas there were an untold number of crazies outside in the woods.

"Well, Mr. New Chick Every Week—" Emilio started, and Becky's head whipped to David. "While we're chatting, I'd like to hedge your bets of them weirdos out there doing their very best to make sure that you never drive out of here again."

"You think I give a shit?" David said. "I expect to take your car, Muscle Mouth."

"Oh really?" said Emilio. "Good luck on an empty tank. You're gonna need it."

"Yeah, maybe jailbait here can push," J.D. grinned as he tapped back into the rapidly deteriorating conversation. "I bet she's been getting lots of practice."

"You mean you two—?" Becky started.

"Disabled the Mazda?" Emilio looked down at her. "Yeah, I guess that must've been us." He turned to David, smiling mockingly. "Nice car."

"I coulda taken a Jag if I wanted to," David protested-slash-bragged. "Maybe I figured a Jag was too good for your class of scum."

"You mean you stole that car?" Becky said as she put it together. "No wonder you didn't seem to care what happened to it."

"For the record, I stole the Mighty Boy as well," David taunted. "You gonna arrest me?"

"You never stopped lying to me, did you?" Becky said.

"And you never stopped talking!" David shot back. He gestured with the shotgun. "On your back!"

"No!" He had lied to her. He had lied to her the whole time. She wasn't going to give him one more centimeter of her false faith in him.

"On your fucking back!" He strode toward her, forcing her back. Finally, she lowered herself to her knees. He liked seeing her like that before him. It was the prettiest she'd ever looked. "Okay, babe, you want to scarf some cock? Be my guest."

"Hey!" Emilio interjected petulantly. "When's it my turn?"

"You couldn't get it up with a crane, numb-nuts," David sneered.

"What about me?" J.D. wanted to know. Always left out. Always coming second. Or third now, somehow. Fuck this guy, David.

"You can blow your buddy here when I'm finished," David told him.

J.D. hated this fucking guy.

Becky steeled herself and reached for the button on David's jeans.

"I'll get that," David said.

"No," she told him, looking up at him from under her eyelashes, her voice deeper. "Let me."

David sneered at Emilio and J.D. as Becky ran her hands up and down David's legs. Then suddenly she clasped her hands together and rammed them upwards right into David's balls. He gasped, dropping the shotgun. Becky quickly snatched it up and got to her feet, turning it first on Emilio and J.D. before pointing it down at David where he huddled on the ground, clutching his throbbing crotch. Speaking of numb-nuts.

"Okay, get off the floor!" she commanded.

"You little slut!" was all she got in reply.

"Enjoy your two buddies over there," she spat at him, corralling him where she wanted with the suggestion of the shotgun's end.

"Becky!"

"No!" she cried. "Just shut up!" She turned to J.D. and Emilio. "Okay, I want to know exactly what's going on. Start talking." She swung the shotgun over toward Emilio. "You!"

"What?" Emilio shot back at her.

"Why did you follow us up here?" Becky demanded.

"Ran J.D. down, didn't he?" Emilio said.

"When?" Becky was getting impatient with all these petulant assholes she was stuck with. What a day.

"This morning."

"He was fucking drunk!" David insisted. "He just didn't see me coming."

"Bullshit, cunt!" J.D. eloquently replied. "You didn't even stop!"

Becky swung the gun back over at David. "Is that right? You didn't stop?"

"Hey, fuck you, Becky!" David said. "You ain't no magistrate."

Maybe not. But right now, she was the one with the fucking gun.

"No, but she's a smarter cookie than you, shithead," Emilio generally despised girls, but right now, he found David far more irritating. This bird was actually sort of interesting. She looked real nice, gripping that gun. He wondered what else she might look nice gripping.

"And you," Becky swung the gun back on Emilio. She was less nice-looking suddenly… "Why didn't you call the police? They would have handled it. Why didn't you do that?"

"Maybe we wanted to handle it ourselves," J.D. said.

"The police wouldn't have done shit anyway," Emilio said.

"So you've been on our tail since this morning," Becky said, then turned on David. "And you've probably known they were behind us all along."

David scoffed at all the accusations. "What of it? It's still none of your fucking business. Why don't you keep your nose out of it?"

"I'm here, aren't I?" she said. "Doesn't that make this whole mess my business too?"

"I can't see how," David pouted.

"David," Emilio butted in. "Not only are you a conniving cheat, you're incredibly stupid. I bet you the other chicks weren't as smart as this one."

"And how come you two seem to know so much about David?" Becky asked.

"We don't. We talked to some kid on the way up here. Taught us a couple of interesting things about old David here."

"What did he tell you?" Becky was mad at herself that she was still a little hurt, about how much she needed to know the full truth. But forget it, she'd already come this far. She deserved to know. And after all, she was the one holding the goddamn gun.

"Hey, why don't you shut up, scum!" David yelled.

"David, don't give me an excuse to fire this thing." Becky nodded back at Emilio. "Go on."

"Well..." Emilio was really relishing this. Physical torture was easy, and something he did commonly. But emotional torture... What a happy, little deviation from the norm. What a way to keep things interesting. And this sure was interesting. "This kid reckons your devoted boyfriend, he brings a new chick up here every Monday."

"Is that right?"

David was so pissed he looked sick. His eyes had taken on a wild, crazed quality, like he knew he'd passed the point of no return, with all of them. "Yeah, and I fuck 'em all too."

"You make me sick," Becky said.

"You make me sick too," Emilio stared at David in disgusted delight.

"And me," J.D. added.

"Shut up, all of you!" Becky said.

"Becky, why don't you put the gun down?" David said, his eyes wet. "Nobody's gonna do anything. I know I'm not. Trust me."

"Trust you?" Becky breathed out. "Trusting you is the biggest mistake I ever made. I'll never trust you again."

"I don't blame you," said Emilio, laying it on thick. "I wouldn't trust him either."

"Shut up, you!" Becky turned her ire on him. "You think

you're any better? You're not. And if there really are people outside, I think you've got a pretty good idea who they are."

"Look, I really wouldn't know," Emilio lied easily.

"Oh really?" Becky countered. "Maybe they followed you up just like you followed us. I don't know what's going on, but I think you do."

"We don't fuckin' know anything," J.D. insisted, lying less well. He couldn't get that little smirk off his face if he tried. He was too amused by all of this.

"I'll believe that when I believe him," Becky scoffed, gesturing at her ex-boyfriend with the shotgun.

"Becky, shut up!"

Becky couldn't believe she ever thought David was clever. *Becky, shut up! Becky, shut up!* What a schoolyard loser with his fucking Fisher Price baby insults.

"And put the gun down!" David demanded, as if he was in the position to do such a thing.

"Yeah, put it down!" Emilio said.

"Yeah, put it down, twat!" J.D. added.

It seems all of them could agree on one thing, which is that they didn't want a girl holding a gun on them or holding their lives in her hands.

Too bad.

"Until I decide whether I want to shoot this thing off or not, just keep your mouths closed tight," she commanded them. *"Okay?"*

They didn't respond.

"I said okay?" she demanded louder.

They refused to answer. That was fine. She would take their silence. As long as she had the gun, she had the upper hand, and as long as she had the upper hand, their silence still meant yes.

CHAPTER 12

"I'LL LIVE TO PISS ON YOUR GRAVE, BITCH!"

Eventually, the orange moon disappeared from the sky, and the posse was on the move again, even more armed than before. A girl in a pink sweatshirt carried a switchblade. Another guy carried an axe. Another kid, a gun. One guy wielded a pitchfork not unlike an angry villager from a Universal Monster Movie. But they weren't on their way to take down Frankenstein's monster. Their targets were much worse. They were not monsters. There was no easy supernatural explanation for what they were and what they did. The good news was, there were no ancient magical tomes to unearth to teach them how to be killed, what their weak spots were. They were men, and they bled just like anyone else. Anywhere.

Finally, the trees cleared, and the posse came upon the cabin. They made quick work surrounding it on all sides, ducking down low so as not to be seen until the right moment. Janie led them, crouching down by the front door.

* * *

Inside, Becky peered out the window, sensing something afoot. Although she had been awake all night, she was alert, still clutching the shotgun in her hands. She wondered if her mother was worried. She wondered if her mother had noticed she was gone at all. Or if she was still out with her boyfriend-slash-boss. If she had come home last night. Becky wondered if she'd be coming home that night herself.

David and J.D. were passed out on the ground in the corner she corralled them into the previous night. Only Emilio was still awake, sulking against the wall, waiting. They all got to their feet quickly enough when she yelled at them to get up.

"You're going outside, okay?" she told them. "You're not staying here."

"We are not going outside!" Emilio yelled back at her.

"You are going outside," she held firm.

"Do you know who's out there?" J.D. wailed.

"I don't care who's out there!" Becky said. "Now, move! *Move!*"

Finally, they did so, heading toward the front door one by one. And she followed them one by one with the barrel of the shotgun.

David hung back a second, like he wasn't sure she really meant him too. But she did. He shuffled toward the door. She glared at him most harshly of all. He had to duck to avoid the barrel she was sticking in his way.

* * *

Outside, Janie clocked the movement within and gestured to her posse to disperse in kind in preparation for attack.

* * *

Emilio stopped suddenly at the door, holding them up.

"Well, what are you waiting for?" Becky asked him. "Get out there."

"I'll live to piss on your grave, bitch!" Emilio said.

J.D. threw her one last somber glare before following Emilio out.

David didn't even look back. That was fine by Becky. She didn't want to look at his useless face ever again.

Becky closed the door behind them and watched through the gauzy curtain that covered the little window in the door as they headed off the porch, like she was watching them through a funeral shroud.

* * *

J.D. grabbed David's ear and yanked him along with them. It was always good to have a back-up plan. J.D. knew enough to know that. He'd watched this documentary on penguins—

Rather he had been forced to watch this documentary on penguins back in school. It happened to be on one of the days he'd bothered to show up. It turned out that penguins were nasty little buggers. If they were hanging out on a chunk of ice, say, and they thought there might be a sea lion in the water nearby, they'd shove one of their own, the weakest one usually, into the water first, and if it didn't get eaten, that meant it was safe to swim off to the next appealing chunk of ice to float around on, and if it did get eaten… Then it meant it wasn't.

David was the weakest penguin. And it would be funny to watch him get eaten. J.D. only wished it was really by a sea lion. Now that would be entertaining.

Footsteps quickened behind them.

Emilio spun around just in time as the girl in the pink sweatshirt came at them with a switchblade. He grabbed the arm holding the switchblade, preventing the knife from finding its mark, and then he knocked her out good. He grinned at where she fell on the ground and kneeled down to finish the job, punching her over and over.

Suddenly, a collective war cry let out. And the posse leapt out from every direction, charging straight at them.

J.D dropped David and ran, not looking back.

Emilio ran off in another direction.

And David in another.

The girl in the pink sweatshirt remained still on the ground.

The rest scattered to chase down their prey, screaming their battle cry all the while.

* * *

Becky watched dispassionately from the window, still clutching the shotgun beside her like her only friend. In a way, it was. It was a killing machine, sure. But it would never lie to her. Its trigger would never refuse to give under her finger if she didn't take her top off first, if she didn't get on her knees. She should ask it to be her boyfriend, she thought. Her mother might even better approve then.

* * *

J.D. and Emilio met back up briefly but then quickly, wordlessly split apart once again, making their own way into the woods.

J.D.'s lungs gave out first. He dropped behind the truck of a large tree, panting desperately.

Emilio's lungs gave out next, and he found his own tree trunk to crouch behind as he caught his breath.

Meanwhile, the posse continued to hunt.

* * *

A little boy found Emilio first. But he was not quick enough. Emilio knocked the kid over onto his back. He was so small, he hardly weighed anything. Emilio saw that the boy dropped something when he went down. There it was now, shining in the morning sun. A machete.

Emilio plucked it up off the ground and embedded it into the little boy's stomach.

From his vantage point crouched behind the tree, J.D. spotted a teenage girl with a hunting knife hunting for him. He came up behind her, knocking her down and forcing her to drop the knife. He straddled her, smacking her once across the face. Then he grabbed the knife and made quick work of slitting her throat. She died quickly, with pain etched now permanently across her face.

He wiped the bloody knife off on his pants, smiling a little, feeling reinvigorated now.

* * *

Nearby in the woods, Christie's brother Mickey had acquired an axe. He caught up with Janie and a few others.

"Come here," Janie beckoned, keeping her voice low but authoritative. "They're on that side okay? So if you just go that way, you that way, and you, come with me."

And then they all ran off on their assignments.

* * *

Nearby, the girl in the Mickey Mouse sweatshirt searched for them. She still held a gun in her small hand.

It didn't help though.

Emilio dropped down out of a tree, smacking the gun out of her hand. Before she knew what hit her, he slashed her twice across the chest, removing Mickey Mouse's world famous ears from the rest of his body. Blood stained his cheery, smiling face.

The face Emilio made down at the gun was similar. He snatched it up, in a better mood already.

* * *

The posse member with the sunglasses who had been standing watch outside the cabin all night found the body of one of his fallen friends, killed senselessly by the marauders, and underneath his sunglasses, his jaw set in grim determination.

* * *

As the rest of them fought, David ran. And David hid.

* * *

A fresh-faced kid readied a slingshot that he'd never use again as Emilio jumped up behind him and plunged a knife into his back over and over again.

* * *

J.D. plunged his own acquired knife into the back of a girl, grabbing up her axe and swinging it into the head of her balaclava-wearing companion, too quickly for him to stop it. It buried itself there easily, making a sound not unlike a kitchen knife stabbed into a watermelon.

* * *

Not knowing where else to go, David headed back to the cabin. He figured he'd sneak his way into the stolen red car while the posse was distracted with the others. Maybe it wasn't so incapacitated as they had claimed. After all, they needed to make a getaway in something, right?

But before he made it around the corner of the cabin, he heard an engine start. He made it just in time to see his getaway vehicle driving away, a single arm and a single finger held out the driver's side window to mock him. David watched it disappear with wide-eyed disbelief.

* * *

Emilio came up behind a few more posse members, singling out the girl bringing up the rear. He grabbed her away from the rest of the group and snapped her neck. She remained still on the forest floor, her mouth gaping open in a silent, unending scream.

* * *

The posse member with the sunglasses permanently attached to his face discovered Christie's body in the rusted out husk of the abandoned car where they'd unceremoniously left her. For now, she would stay there.

He had other graves to dig first.

* * *

Emilio grinned as he came upon the little ginger shit who'd snitched on them in the first place. "Hey, Junior!" He threw the switchblade into the little shit's chest like it was a game of darts. It occurred to him that he should probably take up darts. With an aim like that, he could embarrass lots of drunk idiots, maybe even steal their girlfriends out from under them, they'd be so impressed. But he wasn't looking for any sort of commitment after being cut loose so soon. He wanted to enjoy his singledom. Except... he supposed the baby could use a mother. Perhaps that was something to think about. If it was still alive, that is. Anyway, the boy slid down the tree, futilely clutching the knife stuck in his concave little chest. "That'll teach you to be a little cunt."

Well, it did and it didn't.

Emilio spotted a bleached blonde asshole peering through the trees, looking for them. He was wearing a light blue button-down shirt with a red peace sign painted on one breast. Emilio scoffed at this before aiming the gun right at it. It hit its target. The little hippie groaned and rolled off into a ditch to die. He really should look into his darts idea.

As Emilio headed off to his next kill, J.D. and Emilio finally found each other once again.

"They're fuckin' everywhere!" Emilio exclaimed to his friend, who could only nod in assent.

* * *

Sunglasses met up with Janie and a few others. "Hey, I found that fucking tall guy," he informed them before his attention was snagged on another guy joining them, carrying a coiled length of rope. "Hey, what's the rope for?"

"Maybe it's for hanging him," the guy replied evenly.

Sunglasses liked the sound of that.

With the newfound knowledge of Christie's death, the posse set off after them with renewed purpose, with a reinvigorated bloodlust.

Feeling the winds change, the marauders ran.

CHAPTER 13
"EAT SHIT, SUCKERS!"

J.D. wasn't fast enough. They caught him quick enough. So quick it would have been embarrassing if Emilio had still been there to see. But he had run on.

They dragged J.D.'s bloodied body through the woods until they found a suitable tree.

As he was dragged toward his death, J.D. suddenly realized that while he had fancied himself and Emilio as guerrilla fighters tromping through the woods, it was perhaps these people who were the real guerrilla fighters. They had won, anyway.

The posse all had a hand in setting up the rope, in winding one end of it around J.D.'s neck, in lifting him up, and in watching him hang.

J.D. stuttered and gasped for air that wouldn't come, his legs kicking out for purchase that wouldn't either. At this point, his once bright red underwear was now a dirty, smeared brown.

Emilio was there to see. He crouched in the underbrush nearby. There was nothing he could do but watch.

Sunglasses grinned from the tree he was perched in to hang the rope as he looked down at J.D.'s demise.

Janie got impatient with the slow death. She reached forward, grabbed his belt, and yanked. There was an awful cracking sound, like the breaking of a wishbone, as J.D.'s neck snapped. He hadn't had time to make a wish.

Emilio watched for a beat as J.D. hung there. It looked just like he was asleep. But Emilio knew he wasn't. And then Emilio started moving, figuring this was his chance, now, while they were distracted, awash in the reverence of their righteous kill.

On his first step, he stepped on a branch. It cracked impossibly loud as it broke under his indelicate boot.

Sunglasses heard it right away. He quickly dropped down out of his perch in the tree. The rest of them looked at him in question.

"I saw the other guy," he responded, the call for them to hurry thick in his tone. "Come on!"

They had no other questions.

Emilio ran, making it back to the corroded car that was now Christie's grave. He hid behind the rusted-out hunk of parts as the posse made it to the clearing. Nevertheless, they found him quickly enough, surrounding him on all sides.

There was no place else to hide. Emilio knew this as well as if the big man in the sky himself had come down and whispered it into his cruel ear.

"Eat shit suckers!" Emilio greeted them all. It was as good a last word as any. He raised the pistol in his hands to his mouth.

And then he pulled the trigger.

His thick, dark red blood sprayed over the car, accompanying the hue of the rust and marking it now as a grave for two.

* * *

Back at the cabin, Becky patrolled the front porch, pacing back and forth over the groaning wooden boards, as if they themselves were also under the same duress. Her brow was furrowed with worry, but her eyes were clear and open.

She was too smart to think this was truly over. Not yet.

Because there was one marauder left.

* * *

David screamed as a group of them found him. He ran. They chased him through the woods. They didn't seem to care that he wasn't one of them. They were too high on their own bloodlust now. Insatiable. He ran, frantically trying to make it back to the cabin. Maybe Becky would see. Maybe she would take pity on him. Maybe—

He stopped short as he almost ran headlong into the barrel of the shotgun Becky was holding on him.

The rest of the posse ducked at the sight of the gun.

Only Sunglasses looked up to see what would happen.

David even didn't have time to get a word out before Becky pulled the trigger. The blast threw David back, ripping through his chest, the sound echoing through the now silent woods. *Boom. Boom Boom.* Like a bomb.

Like a reckoning.

Becky looked down dispassionately at David's body, then at the shotgun in her hands. And then she raised her head, staring off into space. A thousand-yard stare in her young eyes. The kind that was usually reserved for war combatants. But she had survived a war now hadn't she?

* * *

Studies have found there is a correlation between heat and violent crime. Reportedly, violent crime increases by up to 5.7% on days with temperatures higher than 85 degrees.

World weather maps have fingered Australia as the hottest place on Earth.

According to NASA, at present, the Earth is warming at a pace of roughly 0.15 to 0.20 degrees Celsius each decade.

Perhaps at some point, most of us will be marauders.

Maybe not.

* * *

The next day, at J.D.'s house, Craig only had a little bit of time to untie his mother and to bring her a rag to clean the dried blood off of her face, while the police knocked louder and louder on the front door.

Fortunately, his mother was well practiced at pretending things were okay even when they weren't, so she greeted the officers with a perfectly believable smile.

When they told her J.D. and his friend were dead, there was nothing left to believe. The smile on her face was real. The tears in her eyes were of relief. But they didn't know that. They offered her words of comfort.

So sorry for your loss, one of them said, without looking up from his little notepad.

God has a plan for everything, the other added dully.

She more or less agreed with the second one.

After they left, she asked Craig, who had just been standing there silently watching, to open the windows. It was stuffy in there. The air stale. She wasn't sure how the request would go over. But Craig simply nodded and went through the house, opening the windows one by one.

She wondered if he would obey her now. If he would be good. If they would be okay. If that's what him opening up all the windows without a fuss signified. But she couldn't be sure. After all, it was 50.7 degrees Celsius outside. 123.3 degrees Fahrenheit. She taught both to her students. She would go to school the next day, as usual. And she would pretend everything was fine. After all, it was just her and Craig now. And he was a good kid. He was. With his brother gone, he would be good now.

And one out of two wasn't that bad.

Right?

* * *

Later, Becky would look up the memorial David had made her wait under. Her initial instincts were sort of correct. It was the Whittlesea War Memorial. The monument had originally been erected to serve as a memorial for Australian soldiers who had fallen during World War II. But as more wars and conflicts lead to more wars and conflicts, they just kept adding names to the bottom of the memorial. Those who had fallen in Korea. And Malaya. And Vietnam. Poor sods who should never have been there in the first place. Who got caught up in other men's thirst for war and bloodshed.

One thing was for certain, on the monument to the conflict that had taken place in the woods, not far off from that very memorial, Becky's name would never be etched.

It had reached 51 degrees Celsius today. 123.8 degrees Fahrenheit. It was the hottest it had ever been. Tomorrow was projected to be even hotter.

Becky closed the windows of her air-conditioned flat.

MARAUDERS PRODUCTION DIARY

The production diary was originally featured in the 2006 DVD release of Marauders by Subversive Cinema. Reprinted here with permission.

ENTRY 1

I have an idea. I'm working full time at a production company doing two or three commercials a week and an industrial. The company owns all its own equipment—cameras, lights, editing suites, production vehicles, etc. The thing is, nobody uses the equipment on weekends; it's just sitting there depreciating. What if I approached the boss and asked him if I could make use of his depreciating assets by making a feature on the weekends? I think I've made enough Super 8 films (over 100), so it's time to go "broadcast".

ENTRY 2

I talked to Paul (Harrington), who camera assists for me, about the project and he has offered to partner up. I spoke to my brother

Colin (Savage), too, and he's also in. Next step is to speak to P**** S******, my boss.

ENTRY 3

Peter is in. Asked what the film was about and I told him very little. Just said it's for the youth market and lovers of nasty films. He doesn't know anything about films, so he simply wished me luck and agreed that the equipment should be utilized for something productive. He just made me agree that shooting the feature wouldn't interfere with my regular directing / shooting gigs. As a surprise, he even gave me a special petrol card for the shoot. What a guy!

ENTRY 4

It's freezing cold here. It's so cold women's nipples are permanently erect.

I am in Noojee, one of Victoria's premier timber towns. I am shooting an industrial for the Victorian Timber Industry Training

Council (VTITC). There is very little to do at night in this place except drink. Since I don't drink, I am retiring to my room each night with a typewriter and writing a script.

The title is *Marauders*. It's the third night of my stay in Noojee and I've written fifty pages. The dialog is flowing nicely and I'm writing a piece that is influenced by *Death Weekend* (aka *House by the Lake*), *Last House on the Left*, and *Straw Dogs*. Because I also love Walter Hill's action films, there is a heavy action-flick bias too.

When I get back to Melbourne, we're going to start casting.

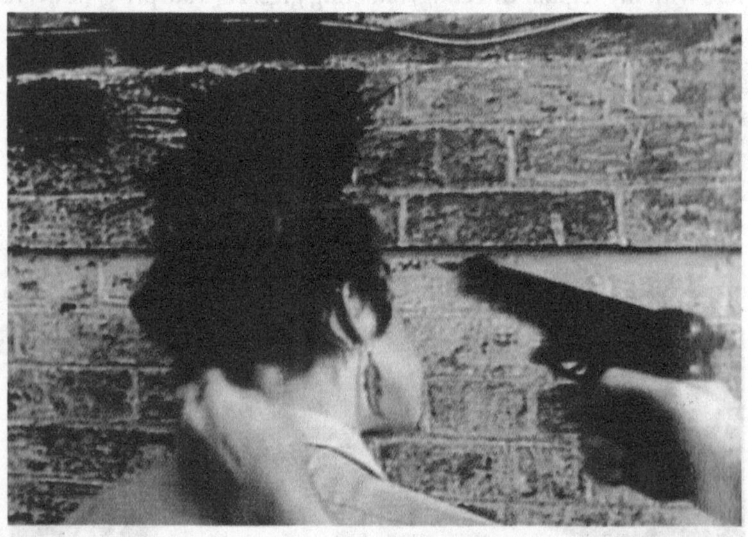

ENTRY 5

The script was finished two weeks ago and everybody has read it. It's pretty straightforward and provides a framework for a film made for exploitation fans BY exploitation fans. Tonight we decided that Colin, my brother, would play Emilio and Paul (Harrington) will play David Frazer. I came up with the name David Frazer because before I started directing commercials for South

Pacific Video, I was a night dubber. That meant I arrived at work every night at 10pm and copied hundreds of VHS and Beta tapes from 1" master tapes until 8am for a variety of clients. The night shift was the only shift that copied X-rated material and, for a while, I was dubbing lots of it. One of my favorites was "Hanky Panky" by Svetlana and David I. Frazer, a really well made, shot-on-film adult flick. Our next job is to cast JD, Emilio's equally psychotic' friend, and Becky, the unfortunate schoolgirl who gets taken for a ride by David Frazer (without the "I").

ENTRY 6

Tonight my wife Susie, who is an excellent cook, offered to cater for the movie. Since it will all be shot over weekends, she will prepare the food and drink on Friday nights for Saturday. Colin has a scene in the movie where he beats up his wife. Since we were running out of possibilities, we asked Colin's girlfriend Sonia if she wanted to play the wife. She agreed.

ENTRY 7

Megan Napier, a young, quiet girl who works with Paul and I at South Pacific, has agreed to take on the role of Becky in *Marauders*. She has also agreed, like everybody else, to dedicate almost nine months of weekends to the project. I visit her at her parents' house in Park Orchards, an outer suburb of Melbourne, and get her to do a line reading as an unofficial audition. She is suitable. Our next casting project is JD.

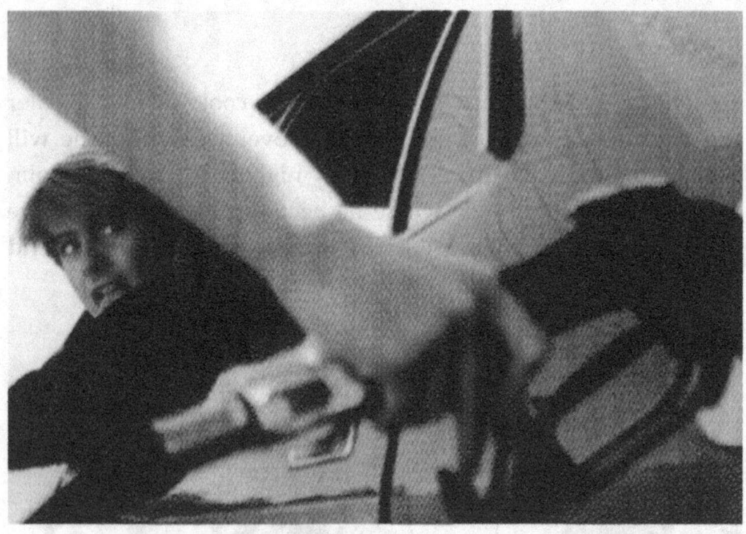

ENTRY 8

Colin, who is a total New Romantic/New Wave devotee, has a friend named Zero (not real name) who has agreed to play JD. I know Zero through Colin, so I'm happy to go with this choice. This morning, Paul and I ask Richard Wolstencroft, a part-time South Pacific employee, if he'd like to be the fourth producer on the project. He said yes. Being a producer on *Marauders* means getting involved in all aspects of pre-production and contributing one-quarter to the cost of broadcast videotapes.

ENTRY 9

Dave B******, a rep for a major tape manufacturer, met me in the parking lot today and sold me a shitload of U-Matic and 1" videotapes. We are shooting on both a Highband U-Matic three-quarter inch recorder and a VPR-5, a portable 1" recorder. Our microphones are a Sennheiser 416 and Sennheiser 816. Our cameras are an Ikegami D and the superior Ikegami E. We're pretty much ready to roll this weekend. Still casting some smaller roles, but our plan is to pre-produce each weekday at night for the coming weekend of shooting. It's not a perfect plan, but since everybody has full-time jobs, it's practical.

ENTRY 10

Just completed first weekend of shooting. Colin bashed his wife, with a spade, and our good friend "Doodoo" has come aboard as key grip. Most of the shooting was done in Northcote, an inner city suburb of Melbourne, and then we moved to Richmond on Sunday where we shot David Frazer in bed with two women. Although it wasn't stated, the two actresses in the scene, Nicole and Nada, are actually sisters. Zero did a long dialog scene with his dead mother that I wasn't too happy with. He's a total party guy and I don't think he'd slept at all on Saturday night. He kept flubbing his lines. While he was doing that, I was thinking of ways to cut around his stumbles. I shot lots of cutaways and then allowed

him to break his dialog up into six pieces. Eventually we got
done.

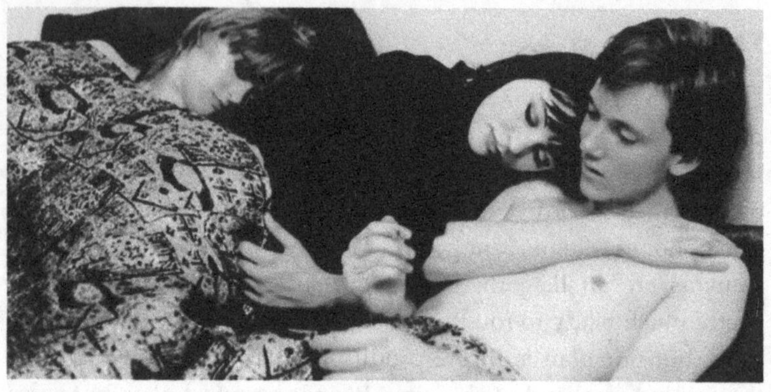

ENTRY 11

We're about four weekends in now.

Yesterday (Saturday) was a nightmare. While we were
shooting Zero walking in front of David Frazer's oncoming car,
Zero misjudged his position and got hit by the car. I was on a
really long lens about two hundred meters away, so the "stunt'
was adequately captured. We even got the port bottle he was
carrying shattering on the road. For about five minutes after the
accident, Zero couldn't move. It was terrible. I thought he was
paralyzed. When he finally got up, he shook himself off and
declared that nothing was broken. But just to be safe, we wrapped
for the day and drove Zero to hospital. They gave him an X-ray
and a doctor checked him out. When the doctor was done, we
proudly showed him the footage of Zero being struck by the car.
He said it made him sick.

ENTRY 12

Still shooting in the city, but ready to shoot in the countryside
next weekend. Everything is going pretty well, although sched-

uling is a problem. Because Paul and I are working so late some evenings for South Pacific, we're getting no time to organize locations and confirm guest actors.

On top of that, some bastards are taking our dedicated production van home on Friday nights if we're not there to stop them. Without a van we're screwed. We lost last weekend because of this.

We've now earmarked someone to save the van for us on Fridays if we're out shooting late. We're paying the opportunistic little bastard a fee for it.

ENTRY 13

Disaster strikes! We've just finished another weekend of shooting, but we may not be shooting ever again. Everybody—Paul, Colin, Richard, Zero, Megan and myself—has formed a tight little family. Since it is Richard's birthday today, we decided to celebrate at Pancakes on the Yarra, a restaurant by the river. When today's shooting was done, we all drove down to the restaurant and parked on the side of the road. About half an hour into the meal we heard a loud and thunderous CRASH! Moments later a guy rushed into the restaurant and asked: "Does anybody here own a blue car or a gold car?" Paul stood up and said that he owned the gold car. I followed and said that I owned a blue one. This guy then asked us to come outside.

What we walked into was a scene of carnage. A Holden Statesman had rounded a curve, left the road, crashed into Paul's car—sending it into the river—then crashed into the rear of my car (with camera equipment in back). For a moment, I was stunned. All I could see was Paul's personal and on-camera car being swallowed by the river and my camera inside its case in the trunk shattered into a million bits. I ran across the road with Paul and looked into my destroyed trunk.

Unbelievably, the trunk had been pushed against the metal camera case. The case could not be damaged. I dragged out the case and inspected the camera, turned it on, rolled tape, played it back and discovered that everything was OK —even the tape that was still in the load mechanism.

Behind us, the drunken bastard who had caused the accident was walking around like an extra from *The Cabinet of Dr. Caligari*. Paul and I both considered punching him. He was so drunk you couldn't even talk to him. The police arrived a few minutes later with a fleet of tow trucks.

ENTRY 14

It's Wednesday night. We've just had an emergency production meeting. The subject of the meeting was: WHAT THE FUCK DO WE DO NOW?

We came up with some options which we now intend to exercise. *Marauders* has a simple story. A guy, David Frazer, picks up his girlfriend, Becky, for a day of banging. On the way, he

ALMOST knocks JD down (that changed to JD DOES knock JD down). JD and Emilio get angry, so they follow David and Becky to take revenge. David and Becky drive onto a ferry that takes them to an island of green-haired weirdos. The men are simpletons and the women have no vaginas. They don't need vaginas because these people don't come from human wombs— they come from the ground where they grow and mature like carrots.

Up until this evening, that was the story. Now it's changed. The plan now is to contact the insurance company of Paul's car and seek permission to roll the car out of the repair shop where it is being assessed so we can shoot a couple of shots of Paul and Megan getting out of it. I will, hopefully, be able to frame the car tightly so we won't see the damage. That will be difficult because there's a lot of damage.

Anyway, from a story point of view, it will be as if they have stopped in a country town for lunch. Then, we will show Colin and Zero approaching the vehicle with sledgehammers as if they intend to destroy it. Next, we will then show Megan pushing the car out of frame and then getting sick of pushing. Paul's solution will be to rent another car. That's the plan, anyway. We can't do any more shooting until Paul's insurance company pays up and he buys a new car.

ENTRY 15

Even though we can't shoot this weekend at all (we're still waiting on permission to shoot Paul's wreck), do you think anybody wanted a break from shooting? No way.

We still got together and shot a dozen perverted comedy skits. We're going to call them *"Magic Men's Favorite Magic."* We shot for a few hours, then got some lunch, shot some more, then got dinner.

I guess we're stuck together for better or worse.

ENTRY 16

Tensions with my wife Susie are a little high. I'm hardly ever home and I'm always working on commercials, industrials or *Marauders*. Even when *Marauders'* people come to visit and hang out at home, Susie feels left out. Which I can understand.

Conducting relationships and being a filmmaker is no easy thing, especially when your films are low budget. This afternoon, Susie and I went out for Dim Sum and had a good time. We came home early and made up for some lost "romance" too (if you get my drift).

When all is said and done, Susie is a real trooper and has been a great caterer. She is a corpse on the floor in Zero's dead mother dialog scene, too. So is my sister Kerri.

ENTRY 17

Paul, who plays David Frazer, has a new car—it is a Suzuki Mightboy, a tiny little craft barely large enough to transport a dwarf. Anyway, it's our new on-camera vehicle. We shot the scenes of Paul and Megan getting out of the wrecked Datsun

today and headed up to Whittlesea to shoot scenes of the Mightboy being "acquired" too. David actually steals the vehicle, but Becky doesn't know that. This weekend, my dad made his appearance in the movie, too. He plays the publican the boys steal liquor from. The storyline has changed now. There is no island of vagina-less women. There are no simpleton men. Now everything is going to take place at my dad's country house in the woods in Kinglake West, an isolated area famous for a few unsolved murders. We'll be doing our own murders there, but nobody will be getting a visit from Mr Plod.

ENTRY 18

Our second rape scene got screwed up today. Anna H******, who we shot before the accident, had played a girl with no vagina whom the boys try to rape. Well, this time Anna played a hitch-hiker who the boys try to rape. During the shooting, Anna tripped and twisted her ankle. It wasn't that bad a twist really, but it gave her an excuse to bow out of the scene (and film).

That left us stranded. We moved to our back-up location and started shooting shots of Emilio and JD lost in the woods. The light was harsh, unfortunately, so it took forever to fill faces and tweak the white balance.

ENTRY 19

Paul and I were invited to a party last night. We accepted the invitation because we needed to find another rape victim amongst the guests. After lots of dead ends, we met Christine, our armorer's girlfriend, a very strong, no-nonsense gal who agreed to do the scene today. It all went very well. The scene will look brutal once cut together, but it was straightforward to shoot and Christine was a real sport about it.

Before we did the scene, Colin asked me if Christine could wear a coat. I asked him why. He said that he needed a coat because he's freezing his balls off. We put Christine in a coat. After the boys dump her body, Colin takes her coat. What a low scumbag!

ENTRY 20

Shooting continues. Around the twenty-eighth weekend and we're still at my dad's house. This weekend the entire cast and crew slept on the location and partied between set-ups. We're doing about sixty set-ups a day and getting tired.

Paul, in addition to doing leading sleazebag chores, is also supervising audio and keeping the camera in good health. Richard, who is in his last year of high school, is not getting much schooling or study done (according to his mother), but he's getting a crash course in film production.

After the shoot this evening, we all convened at South Pacific to watch about five weekends of rushes. It's been impossible to see them lately because there's been some editing going on at the company.

We cut a trailer last night and will show it to the boss during the week. I don't think it will be his bag, but we want to show him that we're not fucking around.

ENTRY 21

Peter S****** watched the trailer today and said, "It's well made, but it's very violent." I expected this response. He's a cool guy, anyway, and I didn't expect him to go nuts for all the blood and violence. He asked Paul and I how much longer we'll be shooting. I estimated about ten more weekends.

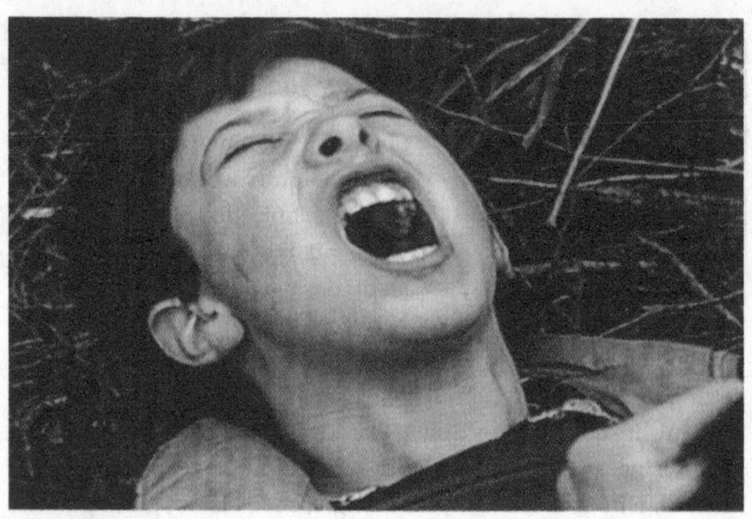

ENTRY 22

The Winter is killing everybody. We've been shooting exteriors for five days now and it's close to freezing all the time. The camera won't fire up some mornings. I have to put it close to the fireplace inside and let the room warm it up.

Susie is still keeping us happy with her food and I was happy that she joined us for the shoot today. She gets along well with everybody and everybody is always nice to the cook.

Next weekend will, hopefully, be the last weekend of exteriors, then we're inside for three weekends and that's it.

ENTRY 23

I'm too tired to type, but I'll give it a try. We did 22 hours straight on Saturday, which meant we wrapped at 6 pm this morning (Sunday). We all crashed on the floor for three hours, then rose again to continue shooting. We shot Colin's suicide and Becky blowing away David Frazer with a shotgun.

Megan had not fired a gun before, so she was rather nervous. Everything went well and Paul died beautifully. Colin's suicide, preceded by the yell, "Eat shit, suckers!", put a smile on everybody's face. I covered the scene from a dozen angles and, as usual, had matching problems with the inconsistent Victorian weather. All up we shot close to forty hours of footage during the production.

ENTRY 24

It's six weeks later now and we've just returned from two days of pick-ups. We added a scene with Colin and Zero and got some sunsets and a perfect full moon (with an 85 filter at night).

Unfortunately, Zero had dyed his hair, but he didn't tell us that on the phone. He just showed up with red hair. Colin's hair was darker, too, so there will some continuity issues.

The film is now cut and is running around seventy-four minutes. We've just off-lined it with two VHS machines connected to a controller. It's a shitty way to cut and I hope it gets easier one day. Every in and out point has to be written down.

Later, we will read all the in/out times to an on-line editor and he will build what's called an EDL (Edit Decision List).

ENTRY 25

On-line editing is underway with a prick of an editor. Because we have no money and he's doing the job as a "favor", he has us over a barrel and is making demands only a Hollywood starlet would make when it's time to order lunch.

Today he ordered three Big Macs, two Apple Pies, two drinks, large fries, a bottle of Coke, and the biggest bag possible of M&M's. Lucky for him we bowed to his prima donna demands.

If only we knew how to use the edit controller ourselves. Our record machines are a VPR-1B and and VPR-2C. My next project is learning the edit system.

ENTRY 26

The on-line is done. Today our composers Mark and John joined us in the edit suite to input their music. Since they had not completed the final twenty minutes of their score, they actually created and played it live into the system as the images danced by. It was amazing to see.

If they screwed something up, our illustrious junk food loving editor would simply back the tape up and roll to re-record so Mark and John could amend their cue.

We were really happy with the result.

ENTRY 27

It's almost a year now since my first diary entry. *"Marauders"* is finished and has been picked up for world distribution by a local sales agent. We screened the film for cast and crew and family and feedback was mostly positive.

My parents enjoyed it, but my mother was offended, not by the raping and killing, but by the use of words like "fuck" and "cunt." She hates swearing more than any other human evil.

ENTRY 28

It's now a year later. Our sales agent has been disappointing.

ENTRY 29

Final entry. *"Marauders"*, though sold to a number of smaller countries, has been pirated in the US, the UK and Germany. There's little we can do about it. We've decided not to pursue further global distribution until the guard changes considerably.